Dear Reader,

I can hardly believe that it is almost twenty years since I wrote my first Harlequin book. The thrill of having that book accepted and then seeing it on the bookshelves—being picked up and chosen by readers—is one I shall never forget.

Twenty years seems a long time. So much has happened during those years; so much has changed and yet so much remains the same. The changes that we have all seen within society are, I believe, reflected in the books we, as Harlequin authors, write. They mirror the changes that take place around us in our own and our readers' lives. Our heroines have changed, matured, grown up, as indeed I have done myself. I cannot tell you how much pleasure it gives me to be able to write of mature—as well as young— women finding love. And, of course, love is something that has not changed. Love is still love and always will be, because love is, after all, an intrinsic, vital component of human happiness.

As I read through these books that are being reissued in this Collector's Edition, they bring back for me many happy memories of the times when I wrote them, and I hope that my readers, too, will enjoy the same nostalgia and pleasure.

I wish you all very many hours of happy reading and lives blessed with love.

Penny Jordan

Back by Popular Demand

Penny Jordan is one of the world's best loved as well as bestselling authors, and she was first published by Harlequin in 1981. The novel that launched her career was *Falcon's Prey*, and since then she has gone on to write more than one hundred books. In this special collection, Harlequin is proud to bring back a selection of these highly sought after novels. With beautiful cover art created by artist Erica Just, this is a Collector's Edition to cherish.

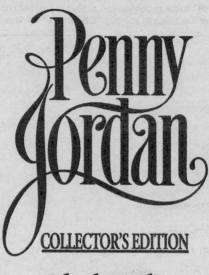

Penny Jordan

COLLECTOR'S EDITION

Blackmail

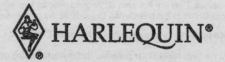

HARLEQUIN®

TORONTO • NEW YORK • LONDON
AMSTERDAM • PARIS • SYDNEY • HAMBURG
STOCKHOLM • ATHENS • TOKYO • MILAN • MADRID
PRAGUE • WARSAW • BUDAPEST • AUCKLAND

ISBN 0-373-63065-4

BLACKMAIL

First North American Publication 1982.

Visit us at www.romance.net

Printed in U.S.A.

ERICA JUST
cover illustrator for the
Penny Jordan Collector's Edition

Erica Just is an artist and illustrator working in various media, including watercolor, pen and ink, and textiles. Her studio is in Nottingham, England.

Her work is inspired by the natural forms, architecture and vibrant colors that she has experienced on her travels, most especially in Africa and India.

Erica has exhibited her work extensively in Great Britain and Europe and has works in private and public collections. As an illustrator she works for a number of companies and also lectures on textile design throughout the country.

CHAPTER ONE

'ARE you okay?'

Lee smiled, her eyes sparkling with anticipation. Her parents had named her, rather foolishly she sometimes thought, 'Annabel-Lee,' but she was 'Lee' to everyone who knew her, a tall, slender girl with long brown hair the colour of beechwoods in autumn, and as glossy as polished chestnuts. Her eyes were green, faintly tip-tilted and fringed with thick curling lashes—witch's eyes, her father had once called them, and her mouth curved generously. No one looking at her mouth could doubt that she had a warm, deeply passionate nature.

Below them the Channel glinted silver in the morning sun. Excitement bubbled up inside her, as frothy and tingling as champagne.

'There'll be a hire car waiting for us at the airport.' Michael Roberts, her boss, told her. 'We'll drive straight down to the Loire.'

Michael was the chief wine buyer for a prestigious supermarket chain and Lee was his assistant. She had been working for him for six weeks, but this was her first 'field trip', so to speak. Michael was in the middle of some delicate negotiations with a wine-grower in the Loire Valley, who so far had been reluctant to allow his *grand* and *premier cru* wines to be sold anywhere but in the most exclusive specialised wine shops. Michael was hoping to persuade him that while these first-class wines should quite rightly continue to be sold to the connoisseur, the English wine-drinking public was growing considerably more discerning and deserved to be able to purchase good wine.

There was considerable rivalry between the various supermarket chains concerning the quality of wines their buyers managed to secure for their customers, and to be able to add the Château Chauvigny label to their range would be a feather in Michael's cap.

After lengthy negotiations the Comte de Chauvigny had invited Michael to visit the vineyards and taste the new wines, and Michael was hopeful that this meant that the Comte was prepared to do business with them.

'At this time of the year we're likely to be the Comte's only guests,' Michael warned Lee, as the seat belt warning lights flashed up, signalling the end of their journey. 'The *grand* and *premier cru* wines will be tasted later in the year by the connoisseurs lucky enough to be able to buy them. What does that fiancé of your's think about you and me flying off to France together?' he asked with a twinkle in his eyes. 'You're quite a career girl, aren't you? How will that tie in with marriage to a Boston Brahmin with a banking empire to inherit?'

'Drew knows how much my career means to me,' Lee said firmly. She had first met her fiancé when she had been working at a vineyard in Australia. They had fallen in love almost at first sight, and there had been little time to discuss such mundane matters as the finer details of their future together. Their time had been short. Lee had already been accepted for her present job, and Drew had been tied up in delicate negotiations for the amalgamation of the banking empire headed by his father, with a Canadian associate.

Until these negotiations were completed there could be no question of their marriage taking place. Drew's family came of Pilgrim stock and their wedding would figure largely in Boston's social calendar. Lee had been a little amused by Drew's insistence that their wedding should be so formal, but had good-naturedly agreed to all Drew's proposals. She frowned slightly as she remembered that it was her turn to phone him. Their transatlantic phone calls were a weekly ritual, and she had already warned Drew that this week's would have to be brief as she would be in France.

The aircraft was descending. Soon they would be landing. She was in France to do a job, Lee reminded herself, and not daydream about her fiancé. Butterflies fluttered in her stomach. This job was important to her and she badly wanted to do well. So far she knew that Michael was pleased with her, so why did she have this vague feeling of anxiety?

Their hire car was a dark blue Renault, and they were going to share the driving. It would take them several hours to reach Chauvigny Michael had warned her. The bright May sunlight touched her hair, burnishing it with gold, and Michael smiled appreciatively. For the journey she was wearing a soft rose-pink linen suit—smart and casual—toned with a cream georgette blouse. She moved with a natural elegance, her legs long and slender as they carried her towards the car.

By mutual consent they had decided not to stop for a meal en route. French lunches were notoriously long-lasting affairs and they had already eaten on the plane. After Orléans Lee took over from Michael. She was a good driver; careful but with enough élan not to be panicked by the French habit of disconcerting overtaking, and soon learned to leave enough room between the Renault and the car in front to allow for any mishaps.

Michael Roberts watched her as she drove, amused by her total concentration. He had never had a female assistant before, but her qualifications and experience had been far superior to those of the other applicants for the job. A wine buyer needs a love of wine; a knowledge of its creation, and most of all that unlearnable ability to discern the superior from the very good, plus a large helping of intuition. The applicants for the job had all been requested to sample several different wines and then make their observations on them. Lee's observations had been far superior to those of the other contenders. She had what was known in the trade as a 'nose'. At first Michael had been dubious about her appointment. Above all else buying wine was a serious business, and who could behave seriously with a beautiful woman like Lee?

Especially Frenchmen, by whom the buying of wine was taken very, very seriously indeed. However, he had soon discovered that his fears were groundless. As his assistant Lee took her duties very seriously; her manner towards their suppliers was as crisp and fresh as a good Muscadet. He had been both amused and pleased by the way she handled the one or two suppliers who had tried to palm her off with an inferior wine. She had given them very short shift indeed, but in such a way that they were never aware that they had been manipulated.

Lee wasn't as unaware of Michael's covert regard as she pretended. Her parents had emigrated to Australia when she was in her first year of university, mainly to be with her brother who had made his home there, and she had very quickly become independent, aware of the fine line which divided a pleasant but casual friendship with members of the opposite sex from something more intimate, and she was equally skilled in making sure that that line wasn't crossed unless she expressly wished it to be. She had been so engrossed in her career that there hadn't been time for serious relationships—until she met Drew. Her parents had been at first amused and then doubtful when she told them what she wanted to do. A school holiday spent in France had sparked off her ambition, and when they realised that she was serious they had done all they could to help her, and now, just when she was realising her first goal, Drew expected her to give it all up. And it wasn't even as though they were to be married yet. It would be some time before he was able to leave Canada, and Lee had planned to save up all her holidays so that they could spend some time together, getting to know one another properly. She glanced at the diamond solitaire on her left hand—discreetly expensive without being flashy; the sort of ring considered appropriate by the Talbot family, no doubt. Dismissing the thought as unfair, she studied their surrounds. Chauvigny was closer to Nantes than Orléans and they were driving through the Loire Valley proper now, past huge châteaux, relics of the time of François I, but it was the vineyards that captured Lee's attention.

In Saumur the valley narrowed, the hills honeycombed with caverns offering wine for sale. At one point the caverns had actually been turned into homes, but the road was too narrow for Lee to give them much attention. They drove through Angers where the Loire widened. Men were working in the vineyards, spraying the precious vines with water to create a protective layer of ice in case of a night frost.

'As soon as they think the frosts are over they'll begin spraying against pests,' Michael told her. 'The recipe for being a good vintner includes such qualities as patience, a thorough understanding of the soil and climate, its benefits and drawbacks, as well as all the complicated processes that go to making a first class wine, plus that indescribable something with which one either is, or is not, born. It can't be learned.'

'We turn off here,' he instructed, indicting a steep right fork off the main road.

They climbed steadily through gently rolling hills,

flattening out in the distance to Nantes and the coast, vines growing on either side of the road; through a small, almost mediaeval village, and then the château was in front of them, the smooth cream walls rising out of the still waters of a moat, fairy-tale spires, shining pale gold against the azure evening sky, the whole thing so impossibly beautiful, like a mirage floating on a calm oasis, that Lee could not understand why she felt this renewed sensation of nervous apprehension spiralling through her.

'Well, well, it looks like the real thing,' Michael commented, obviously impressed. 'When a Frenchman talks about a château it can be anything from a country cottage to Buckingham Palace. It looks as though this one really meant it. All it needs is Errol Flynn to come flying through the window to complete the Hollywood image!'

A permanent 'drawbridge' spanned the moat; the Renault disturbed two elegant swans who had been gliding slowly below. Odd how such graceful water birds could look so clumsy on land, Lee thought absently, watching them.

The drawbridge gave way to an arched gateway, beyond which stretched an enclosed courtyard. She had seen homes equally impressive in Australia, she reminded herself, trying not to be quelled by the château's air of ancient grandeur, coupled with an aura of discreet wealth. Wisteria blanketed the cream walls, racemes of purple-blue flowers smothering the gnarled branches, reminiscent in shape and size of the bunches of grapes themselves.

The sound of the car alerted the dog who had been sleeping in front of the large double doors. Lee stopped the car and wound down the window. The evening air was clean and fresh after the staleness of the Renault. She could hear the sound of water, and as her eyes grew accustomed to the creeping shadows she saw the shallow stone basin with its fountain, a boy holding—not a water jar, but a bunch of grapes from which sprang the droplets which filled the basin beneath, sparkling like champagne.

Tubs of geraniums and lobelia added a colourful splash to the cobbled courtyard, and as she looked about her, Lee realised that they were at the back of the château in what had probably once been the stables and outbuildings. She looked up at the house. Blank windows stared back at her, the circular towers she had noticed from the road having only narrow arrow slits, proclaiming their great age.

The double doors opened, the dying sun blinding Lee momentarily as it was reflected in the leaded windowpanes. A man emerged from the château dressed in an expensively tailored dove grey suit, his black hair brushed back off a face which was stamped with the indelible marks of centuries of breeding. He spoke sharply to the dog, which was still barking noisily, a wolfhound almost as high as the lean hips encased in the pale grey mohair. Nervous tension crawled sickeningly through Lee's body, causing her hands to lock whitely on the steering wheel. Michael climbed out of the car and opened her door. She followed him on legs which suddenly seemed to have turned to cotton wool.

'Michael Roberts,' Michael announced, introducing himself, 'and my assistant,' he turned to Lee and smiled, 'Lee Raven, and you, of course, must be…'

'Gilles Frébourg, Comte de Chauvigny.'

He spoke perfect, accentless English—but then of course he always had, Lee thought numbly, battling against the shock that had locked her muscles in mute protest, the moment she looked into—and recognised—his arrogant features. After all, his mother *was* English.

'Lee.'

His pronunciation of her name betrayed none of her shock. The hand he extended towards her was tanned, the fingers lean, his grip powerful.

'Gilles.' She murmured his name in the same perfunctory tone he had adopted, adding carelessly, 'How is Aunt Caroline?'

His eyes gleamed, as though he was well aware that beneath her calm words lurked nerve-racking chaos.

'Very well, and enjoying the Caribbean. Lee and I share an aunt in common,' he explained to Michael, who was looking increasingly baffled. 'Or at least, she is my aunt and…'

'My godmother,' Lee supplied, taking a deep breath and willing herself to appear calm. Talk about coincidence! She had never dreamed when she left England that their destination was also the home of Gilles Frébourg. And if she had nothing would have brought her within a thousand miles of it, she thought with a bitter smile.

'Come inside.' Gilles' smile mocked her, as though he had read her mind. 'My housekeeper will show you to your rooms. Tonight we do not dine formally, as it is your first in my home. I am sure you must be tired and will perhaps want an early night. Tomorrow we shall tour the vineyards.'

Thin gold slats of sunshine touched precious antiques, as they stepped into a vast square hall, its floor covered in a carpet so soft and beautiful that it seemed criminal to walk on it. The Chauvigny arms were cut in stone above the huge fireplace, and Lee remembered now, when it was too late, Aunt Caroline mentioning that her sister's brother-in-law was a Comte.

They had all been at school together, her mother, Aunt Caroline, and Aunt Caroline's sister, Gilles' mother, although she, of course, had been several years older than the other two. Lee glanced at Gilles. It was almost six years since she had last seen him. He hadn't changed, unless it was to become even more arrogantly male. Did he find her altered? He must do, she reflected. She had been sixteen the last time they met, shy, gawky, blushing fiery red every time he even looked at her, and now she was twenty-two with a patina of sophistication which came from living alone and managing her own affairs. That summer when she had met Gilles he had been staying with his aunt, following a bad bout of 'flu. He had been twenty-five then.

The housekeeper, introduced as Madame Le Bon,

was dressed in black, plump hands folded over the front of her dress as she obeyed Gilles' summons, cold eyes assessing Lee in a way which she found unnerving.

There was a portrait facing them as she and Michael followed the woman upstairs. The man in it was wearing the uniform of Napoleon's hussars, but the lean body beneath the dashing uniform and the face below the tousled black hair—worn longer, admittedly, than Gilles'—were quite unmistakably those of their host. Even Michael was aware of the resemblance, for he drew Lee's attention to it as they passed beneath the huge painting. The man in the portrait seemed to possess a rakish, devil-may-care quality which in Gilles had been transmuted into a careless arrogance which Lee found less attractive, and which seemed to proclaim to the world that its opinion of him mattered not one jot and that he was a man who lived only by rules of his own making. A man whom it would be very, very, dangerous to cross—but then she already knew that, didn't she?

'You are on the same floor,' the housekeeper told Michael and Lee. 'If you wish adjoining rooms…'

Lee felt the colour burn along her cheeks at the manner in which the woman quite deliberately posed the question. She glanced at Michael, pointedly.

'Miss Raven and I are business associates,' he pointed out very firmly. 'I'm sure that whatever has been arranged will be admirably suitable. Adjoining rooms are not necessary.

'Not that I wouldn't want to share a room with

you,' he told Lee a little later when he had settled in and come to see how she was progressing with her own unpacking. Her bedroom faced out on to the formal gardens in front of the château, although with the dusk creeping over them it was impossible to make out more than the shadowy outlines of clipped hedges, and smell the scent of early flowers. 'Always supposing you were willing, which I know quite well you're not, but it doesn't say much for the morals of our countrymen and women, does it? Perhaps they've had a surfeit of visitors with "secretaries",' he added with a grin.

It could well be that Michael was right, Lee reflected, but there had been something about the way the housekeeper had looked at her when she had spoken which had made Lee feel that the remarks had been directed specifically towards herself. Her eyes narrowed thoughtfully.

'You never told me you had connections in high places,' Michael teased. 'Had I known you knew the Comte personally we needn't have bothered coming down here. You could have used your influence to get him to agree.'

'I didn't know he had inherited the title,' Lee told him. 'As you've probably guessed, our relationship, if you can call it that, is very tenuous, and there's certainly no blood connection. I've only met him once before. I couldn't even call us acquaintances.'

But there was more to it than that—much more, Lee reflected when Michael had left her to finish her unpacking and change for dinner. Such as her foolish

sixteen-year-old self imagining she was in love with
Gilles. It must have been the crush to beat all crushes.
A small private boarding school where many of the
girls were the daughters of strict Spanish and South
American parents was not the ideal place to gain an
adequate knowledge of sexual matters. She had been
greener than grass; completely overwhelmed by the
powerful attraction she felt for Gilles. Had he asked
her to lie down and die for him no doubt she would
have done so. Her infatuation had been of the order
that asks no more of the beloved being than merely
that he existed. There had been no sexual awareness
in her adoration apart from that which goes hand in
glove with a girl's first love. She put it all behind her
long ago, especially its grubby, sordid ending, which
had done so much to sully her memories of that year.

Her bedroom was vast. Their visit to the château
was to be a short one—three days—which would allow them to see the vineyards, the cellars where the
wine was stored, and still allow some time for the
negotiations which Michael hoped would result in
them securing the Chauvigny label for Westbury's.
She wondered if she ought to alert Michael to the fact
that her being his assistant might seriously detract
from his chance of doing so, and then decided against
it. She was remembering Gilles with the eyes of a
sixteen-year-old child. It was surely hardly likely that
an adult male of thirty-one would bear a grudge
against a child of sixteen.

Gilles certainly believed in treating his guests lavishly, she reflected, hanging the neat, understated ton-

ing separates she had brought with her in the vast
fitted wardrobes which lined one wall of the room,
their fronts mirrored and decorated with delicate panel
mouldings to match the rest of the bedroom, which
was furnished with what she suspected were genuine
French Empire antiques. It wasn't hard at all to imagine a provocatively gowned Josephine reclining on
the pale green satin-covered chaise-longue, waiting
impatiently for her lover.

Everything in the room matched; from the self-
coloured design on the pale green silk wall coverings,
to the curtains and bed covers.

A beautiful ladies' writing desk was set beneath the
window with a matching chair; the dressing table was
French Empire, all white and gold with delicate spin-
dly legs, the table lamps either side of the huge double bed the only modern touch, but even these might
have been made for this room.

Lee wasn't a fool. The furnishing in this room—
from the precious silks down to the faded but still
beautiful pale green and pink carpet which she suspected must be Aubusson—must surely be worth a
king's ransom; and this was only one of the château's
many rooms. Gilles must obviously be a very wealthy
man; a man who could afford to pick and choose to
whom he sold his wine. No doubt after the vintage
he would hold those dinner parties for which French
vignerons are so famous, when the cognoscenti gathered to partake of lavish dinners conducted in formal
surroundings, all carefully designed as a paean of trib-
ute to the evening's guest of honour—the wine.

This was the first time Lee had visited such an exclusive vineyard. In Australia, where she had spent a year working alongside a grower in his own vineyards, things were much more casual, in keeping with the young vigour of their wines. Now she was grateful for the momentary memory of her teenage visit to a French vineyard which had urged her to pack a slender sheath of a black velvet dress.

Her bedroom had its own private bathroom; so blatantly luxurious that she caught her breath in bemusement as she stared first at the sunken marble bath and then the gold fittings. Even the floor and walls were marble, and she felt as decadent as a harem girl whose one desire in life was to pleasure her master, as she sank into the deep, hot water and luxuriated with abandoned delight. In London she shared a flat with two other working girls, and there was rarely time for more than a workmanlike shower, and the odd long soak when she had the flat all to herself.

Lifting one long, slender leg from the suds, she eyed it dispassionately. Gilles certainly knew how to live. Why had he not married? Surely a home and responsibilities such as his must make the production of a son and heir imperative, and Frenchmen were normally so careful in these matters. He was, after all, thirty-one. Not old…she laughed aloud at the thought of anyone daring to think such a vigorous and aristocratic man as Gilles old. Even when he did eventually reach old age he would still be devastatingly attractive. She frowned. Where were her thoughts

leading her? Surely she was not still foolish enough
to feel attracted to Gilles?

She got out of the bath and dried herself slowly.
Of course she was not; she had learned her lesson.
She glanced towards the telephone by her bed. She
would ring Drew. Michael had assured her that she
might, and that he would ensure that the call was paid
for.

It didn't take long to get through. Drew's Boston
accent reached her quite clearly across the miles that
separated them. He sounded rather brusque, and Lee's
heart sank.

'You decided to go, then?'

His question referred to the fact that he had not
been pleased to learn that she was due to travel abroad
with Michael. In fact he had tried very hard to dis-
suade her, and they had come perilously close to their
first quarrel. Now, squashing her misgivings, Lee replied firmly, 'It's my job, Drew—you know that. You
wouldn't expect me to make a fuss because you have
to work in Canada, would you?'

There was a pause, and then Drew's voice saying
coldly, 'That's different. There's no need for you to
work at all, Lee. As my wife you'll be expected to
fulfil certain duties. You should be spending these
months before our marriage in Boston. Mom did in-
vite you.'

So that she could be vetted as to her suitability to
marry into such a prominent family, Lee thought resentfully.

'So that she could make sure I don't eat my peas

off my knife?' she remarked sarcastically, instantly wishing the words unsaid as she caught Drew's swiftly indrawn breath.

'Don't be ridiculous!' He sounded stiff now, and angry. 'All Mom wanted to do was to introduce you around the family. When we're married we'll be living in Boston, and it will help if you already know the ropes. Mom will propose you to the charity committees the family work for, and...'

'Charity committees?' Once again Lee's hot tongue ran away with her. 'Is that how you expect me to spend the rest of my life Drew? I already have a career...'

'Which takes you gallivanting all over the place with other men. I want my wife at home, Lee.'

All at once she understood. He was jealous of Michael! An understanding smile curved her mouth. How silly of him! Michael was in his late forties and well and truly married. All at once she wished the width of the Atlantic did not lie between them, but she had already been on the phone for several minutes. She glanced at her watch and said hurriedly, 'Drew, I can't talk any more now. But I'll write soon...'

She hoped he would say that he loved her, but he hung up without doing so, and she told herself it had probably been because someone might have overheard. It was too late now to regret those impetuously hasty words. She could only hope that her letter would mollify him. There wasn't time to start it before dinner, and she tried to put the whole thing out of her mind until later. The black dress set off her creamy skin, still holding the faint sheen of her Australian tan. The neckline, high at the throat, plunged to a deep vee at the back, exposing the vulnerable line of her spine, drawing attention to the matt perfection of her flesh. Long sleeves hugged her arms to the wrists, the skirt skimming her narrow hips, a demure slit revealing several inches of thigh, now encased in sheer black stockings. Her mother had been with her when she bought the dress, and it was she who had suggested the stockings. 'Something about that dress demands them,' she had insisted firmly. 'It's a wicked, womanly dress that should only be worn when you're feeling particularly female, and with it you must wear the sheerest stockings you can find.'

'So that every man who sees me in it will know just what I'm wearing underneath it?' Lee had exclaimed, scandalised. She had already realised that there was just no way she could wear a bra with the dress, and now her mother, of all people, was suggesting that she go a step farther!

'So that every man who sees you in it will *wonder* what you're wearing,' her mother had corrected. 'And hope he's right! Besides,' she concluded firmly, 'there's something about wearing stockings which will make you feel the way you ought to feel when you're wearing that dress.'

It had been impossible to argue with her mother's logic, but now Lee wasn't so sure. The fine Dior stockings enhanced her long, slim legs, the velvet

sumptuous enough on its own, without any jewellery.
On impulse, Lee swept her hair into a smooth chignon, leaving only a few softening wisps to frame her
face. All at once her eyes seemed larger, greener, the
classical hairstyle revealing her perfect bone structure.
When she looked in the mirror she saw not a pretty
girl, but a beautiful woman, and for a moment it was
almost like looking at a stranger. She even seemed to
be moving more regally. She applied the merest hint
of green eyeshadow, a blusher frosted with specks of
gold, which had been a hideously expensive Christmas present from her brother and which gilded her
delicately high cheekbones to perfection, then added
a lip gloss, darker than her daytime lipstick. Perfume—her favourite Chanel completed her preparations and then, slipping on the delicately heeled black
sandals, she surveyed her reflection in the mirror,
rather like a soldier preparing for a hard battle, she
admitted wryly.

Michael whistled when he saw her.

'What happened?' he begged. 'I know Cinderella
is supposed to be a French fairytale, but this is ridiculous!'

'Are you trying to tell me that I arrived here in
rags?' Lee teased him.

'No. But I certainly didn't expect the brisk, businesslike young woman I left slightly less than an hour
ago would turn into a beautiful seductress who looks
as though she never does anything more arduous than
peel the old grape!'

Lee laughed; as much at Michael's bemused expression as his words. The sound ran round the enclosed silence. A door opened and Gilles walked towards them. Despite his claim that they would dine informally he was wearing a dinner suit, its impeccable fit emphasising the lean tautness of his body. Lee was immediately aware of him in a way that her far more naïve sixteen-year-old self had never been. Then he had dressed in jeans and tee-shirts, or sometimes when it was hot, just jeans, and yet she had never been aware of his body as she was now; the muscular thighs moulded by the soft black wool, the broad shoulders and powerful chest; the lean flat stomach.

'Do you two have some means of communication I don't know about?' Michael complained. 'I thought we were dining informally?' He was wearing a lounge suit, and Gilles gave him a perfunctory smile.

'Please forgive me. I nearly always change when I am home for dinner. The staff expect it.'

Lee stared at him. From her estimation of him she wouldn't have thought he gave a damn what the staff expected.

'It is necessary when one employs other people to make sure that one has their respect,' he said to her, as though he had guessed her thoughts. 'And there is no one quite so snobbish as a French peasant—unless it is an English butler.'

Michael laughed, but Lee did not. God, Gilles was arrogant—almost inhuman? Did he never laugh, cry, get angry or make love?

The last question was answered sooner than she

had expected. They were in what Gilles described as the 'main salon', a huge room of timeless elegance of a much older period than her bedroom. Louis Quatorze, she thought, making an educated guess as she studied a small sofa table with the most beautiful inlaid marquetry top. Gilles had offered them a drink, but Lee had refused. She suspected that only house wines would be served during dinner and she did not want to cloud her palate by drinking anything else first. Neither of the two men drank either, and she would feel Gilles watching her with sardonic appraisal. He was a man born out of his time, she thought, watching his face. Why had she never seen before the ruthless arrogance, the privateer, the aristocrat written in every feature?

The door opened to admit Madame Le Bon. She gave Gilles a thin smile.

'*Madame est arrivée.*'

Who was the woman who was so well known to Gilles' household that she was merely referred to as Madame? Lee wondered. Gilles did not move, and Lee could almost feel the housekeeper's disapproval. She looked at Lee, her eyes cold and hostile, leaving Lee to wonder what she had done to merit such palpable dislike, and all on the strength of two very brief meetings—and then she forgot all about the housekeeper as another woman stepped into the room. She was one of the most beautiful women Lee had ever seen. Her hair was a rich and glorious red, her skin the colour of milk, shadowed with purple-blue veins. Every tiny porcelain inch of her shrieked breeding, right down to the cool, dismissing smile she bestowed upon Michael and Lee.

'Gilles!'

Her voice was surprisingly deep, a husky purr as she placed one scarlet-tipped hand on Gilles' arm and raised her face for a kiss which, her seductively pouted mouth informed the onlookers, was no mere formality.

The scarlet, pouting mouth was ignored, and to Lee's surprise Gilles lifted her hand to his lips instead. Perhaps he was embarrassed about kissing her in front of them, she deduced, although she had thought him far too arrogant to mind about that.

'Forgive me for not dressing more formally,' she purred, indicating the sea-green chiffon gown which Lee was quite sure came from one of the famous couture houses. 'But I have only this afternoon returned from Paris. And these are your guests...'

Gilles introduced them.

'Louise—Lee Raven, and Michael Roberts. Madame Beauvaise. Her father is my closest neighbour. Another wine grower...'

Louise's lips pouted, her eyes narrowing slightly as she scrutinised Lee, so thoroughly that Lee felt there wasn't anything about her which had not been inspected and priced—including her stockings.

'Come, *chéri*,' she protested lightly, 'you make it sound so formal and dull. We are more to each other than mere neighbours, you and I. And you, Miss Raven—you are wearing a betrothal ring, I see. Do we take it that you and Mr Roberts are to marry?'

First the housekeeper and now this woman; there seemed no shortage of people willing to thrust her into Michael's arms, it seemed.

'No, we are not,' she said shortly, not prepared to elucidate. There had been a suggestiveness behind the Frenchwoman's words which she had disliked intensely; it had almost been that of a voyeur, distasteful though the thought was, and for the first time Lee saw the sensuality behind the redhead's elegant poise, the greedy hunger of her mouth as it parted suddenly when she looked at Gilles. Feeling faintly sick, Lee wished she could escape to her room. There was something about Louise which reminded her of a particularly deadly species of orchid, all dazzling beauty on the surface, but underneath...poisonous.

The meal was as delicious as Lee had envisaged—soup served with a perfect, dry rosé which cleansed the palate; deliciously tender lamb with a full-bodied red which brought out the subtle flavour of the roast meat, and finally a cheese board with a choice of Rocamadour, Picodon, and Charolles, all chosen to complement the dry, fruit white wine.

Michael was a skilled raconteur, and the talk around the dinner table was general and light, only Louise pouting occasionally as though longing to be alone with the man Lee now no longer had any doubt was her lover. It was there in every look she gave him, the constant touch of her fingers on his arm; the intimate possessive glances which said quite plainly, this man is mine.

After dinner they returned to the salon. The house-

keeper brought in the coffee; like the dinner service
the cups were beautiful porcelain, and had not, Lee
suspected, been purchased from any store.

Louise got up gracefully to pour the coffee, but to
Lee's amazement Gilles restrained her.

'Perhaps Lee will be mother?' he suggested with a
slight inclination of the arrogant dark head. Lee was
astounded, but such was the authority of his voice that
it never occurred to her to refuse.

The hauteur with which Louise surveyed her almost made her laugh out loud.

'Mother?' she repeated disdainfully.

'An English expression,' Gilles informed her. 'I
should have mentioned it earlier, but Lee and I are
old friends. We have an aunt in common.' He reached
for Lee's hand as he spoke, such a look of tender
amusement in his face that she almost caught her
breath in disbelief.

Louise seemed to share her bemusement. She was
staring from Lee to Gilles with narrowed eyes, her
face no longer beautiful, but hard and dangerous.

'I hope that as such an old friend, Lee will not mind
sharing you with…newer friends…'

There was a warning as well as a question in the
silky words, and Lee realised with a sense of shock
that the redhead actually thought she might be a con-
tender for Gilles' affections. As though she would
attempt anything so foolish!

She was even further astonished when Gilles carried her fingers to his lips, an expression which in

anyone else might almost have been called doting, in the slate-grey eyes, now warm and smouldering.

'Well, darling?' he enquired in tones of deepest affection. 'Will you be jealous of my old friends?'

'Darling?'

For a moment Lee thought she had been the one to say the word, and then a look at Louise's furious white face informed her that although they had heard the endearment with equal shock, the Frenchwoman had been the first to announce her shock verbally.

Lee glanced at Michael to see what he was making of all this strange behaviour on the part of their host, but he was simply relaxing in his chair, a small smile playing round his lips as he waited for the explosion none of them were in any doubt was imminent. Unless of course it was Gilles, who was looking for all the world as though there was no reason why he should not call Lee 'darling' in front of his mistress, and none at all why she should resent it. That look of icy hauteur would certainly have been enough to make her think twice about creating a scene, Lee reflected uncertainly, but then perhaps she had more experience of exactly how brutal Gilles could be when he wanted to than the infuriated Frenchwoman.

'Isn't that how one normally addresses a fiancée?' Gilles murmured smoothly.

'A... You mean...'

'Lee and I are engaged to be married,' he agreed silkily, obviously realising that while Louise had grasped the meaning of his words, she was, as yet, incapable of vocalising her reaction to them.

'She is not wearing the Chauvigny betrothal ring.'

'A small omission,' Gilles said coolly. 'It has been an understood thing between us for many years that we should marry, but on my last visit to England I found her so grown up and…desirable that I could not wait to…seal our betrothal. Since I do not carry the Chauvigny emerald around with me—which I am sure, my dear Louise, you will have already marked, will match Lee's eyes exactly—I had to make do with this small trifle.'

Drew's diamond was removed from Lee's finger before she could protest, Gilles shrugging aside Louise's impatient questions as though he found them both boring and impertinent. After a long tirade in French which Lee was mercifully relieved that she could not understand, the redhead got up and stalked over to her, eyes venomous as they stared down into her oval face.

'You may have made this innocent your betrothed, Gilles—do not think I do not know why. The woman who gives birth to the Chauvigny heir must of course be above reproach, but she will never bring you the pleasure in bed that I did. She will have milk and water in her veins, your English bride, not blood. And as for you…' her eyes swept Lee's pale face. Events were moving much too fast for Lee. She ought to have denied Gilles' statement right from the start, but she had been far too stunned, and he, taking advantage of her bemusement, had spun a tale around them which pointed to him being a skilled and resourceful liar.

'Do you really think you will keep him?' Louise demanded scornfully. 'How long will it be before he leaves your bed for someone else's, in Paris or Orléans, while you are left to sleep alone? Look at him!' she insisted. 'He is not one of your cold, passionless Englishmen. He will take your heart and break it as he did mine, and feed the pieces to the vultures. I wish you joy of him!'

Gilles, looking unutterably bored, held open the door as she stalked towards it, and through it, leaving a silence behind her which could only be described as deafening.

CHAPTER TWO

'AND what,' Lee asked dangerously, when the front door had slammed behind the furious Frenchwoman, and Michael had discreetly left them to it, 'was all that about?'

Far from looking ruffled, Gilles appeared enviably calm—far calmer than she was herself. He lit a thin cheroot with an expensive gold lighter, studying the glowing tip for a few seconds before replying coolly,

'I should have thought it was obvious. You are not, I think, lacking in intelligence. You must surely have observed that Louise considered her position in my life far more important than it actually was.'

His sheer arrogance took Lee's breath away.

'An impression which you of course did nothing to foster!' she smouldered, too furious now for caution. Of all the hypocritical, arrogant men! To actually dare to use her to get rid of his unwanted mistress!

'Louise knew the score,' he replied emotionlessly. 'If she decided she preferred being the Comtesse de Chauvigny, rather than merely the Comte's mistress, it is only natural that I should seek to correct her erroneous impression that she may step from one role to the other merely on a whim.'

'Her place is in your bed, not at your side, is that what you're trying to say?' Lee seethed. Really, he was quite impossible! 'She was good enough to sleep with, but...'

'You are talking of matters about which you know nothing,' Gilles cut in coldly. 'In France marriage is an important business, not to be undertaken without due consideration. Louise's first husband was a racing driver, who was killed during a Grand Prix; for many years she has enjoyed the...er...privileges of her widowhood, but a woman of thirty must look to the future,' he said cruelly, 'and Louise mistakenly thought she would find that future with me. A Chauvigny does not take for a bride soiled goods.'

Lee made a small sound of disgust in her throat and instantly Gilles' eyes fastened on her face.

'You think it a matter for amusement?' he demanded. 'That a woman such as that, who will give herself willingly to any man who glances her way, is fit to be the mistress of this château?'

'She was fit to be yours,' Lee pointed out coolly.

Hard grey eyes swept her.

'My mistress, but not my wife; not the mother of my children. And before you say anything, Louise was well aware of the position. Do you think she would want me if it were not for the title, for this château?'

'Possibly not.' Now what on earth had made her say that? Lee wondered, watching the anger leap to life in Gilles' eyes. What woman in her senses would not want Gilles if he owned nothing but the clothes he stood up in? The thought jerked her into an awareness of where such thoughts could lead. What woman would? she demanded of herself crossly. Certainly not her, who knew exactly how cruel and hateful he could be!

'I am not interested in your emotional problems, Gilles,' she told him firmly. 'What I want to know is why you dared to drag me into all this, or do you still enjoy inflicting pain just for the thrill of it?'

There was a small silence when it would have been possible to hear a pin drop, had such an elegant room contained so homely an object; a time when Lee was acutely conscious of Gilles' cold regard, and then, as the silence stretched on unnervingly, she held her breath, frightened, in spite of her determination not to be, by the hard implacability in Gilles' face.

'I will forget that you made that last remark. As to the other—' he shrugged in a way that was totally Gallic, 'because you were there, because we are known to one another; because you were already wearing a betrothal ring which made things so much easier.'

'Well, as of now,' Lee told him through gritted teeth, as she listened in appalled disbelief to his arrogant speech, 'our betrothal is at an end!'

'It will end tomorrow,' Gilles told her arrogantly, as though she had no say in the matter. 'When we marry.'

'*Marry?*' Lee stared at him. 'Have you gone mad? I wouldn't marry you if you were the last man on earth! Have you forgotten that I'm engaged to another man? A man whom I love, and who loves me…'

'But who does not trust you,' Gilles drawled succinctly. 'Otherwise he would not have telephoned here this morning to ask if you had arrived, and if you were to share a room with Michael Roberts. I confess I was intrigued to meet you again; you must have changed considerably, I told myself, to arouse such jealousy.'

Lee ignored the subtle insult. He had known she was coming, then. Had that scene with Louise all been planned? She didn't want to think so, but knowing Gilles, it was just the sort of Machiavellian action he would delight in.

'Sit down,' he instructed her coolly, grasping her shoulders with cool hands, tanned, with clean, well cared for nails. Hands which held a strength that bruised as he forced her into a brocade-covered chair, which alone was probably worth more than the entire contents of her small flat. 'Before you lay any more hysterical charges at my feet, allow me to explain a few facts to you.

'Louise's father is a close friend of mine, and a neighbour, whom I greatly respect. Louise has completely blinded him as to her true personality, and out of charity his friends keep silent as to her real nature. He owns lands which borders mine, fine, vine-growing land, which will eventually form Louise's *dot* should she remarry, but Bernard is growing frail and can no longer tend this land himself. I should like to buy it from him…'

'Why don't you simply marry Louise?' Lee butted in, too furious to stay silent any longer. 'Then you'll get it for free.'

'On the contrary,' Gilles said smoothly, 'I shall have to pay a very heavy price indeed. The price of knowing that my wife is known intimately to every other man in the neighbourhood who has glanced her way; the price of not knowing whether I have fathered any children she may bear. However, I now discover that our names have been linked by local gossip— gossip deliberately fed by Louise, I am sure, for she would stop at nothing to become my wife.'

Again his arrogance took Lee's breath away, but before she could protest, Gilles was continuing emotionlessly.

'I had two choices open to me. Either I must give in to Louise's blackmail, or cause great pain to an old friend.'

'And thereby lose his rich land,' Lee commented sotto voce, but Gilles ignored her.

'However, on this occasion I was presented with a third, and infinitely preferable choice—marriage to someone else, a marriage which will calm Bernard's suspicions, silence Louise's malicious tongue, and far more important, a marriage which can be set aside when its purpose has been achieved. In short, my dear Lee, a temporary marriage to you.'

Lee was lost for words. She stared at him, her green eyes wide with disbelief.

'I won't do it,' she said positively, when she had found her voice. 'You can't make me, Gilles.'

'Oh, but I can,' he said silkily.

He walked across the room, removing a small key from several on a key ring which he returned to his pocket, then unlocked a beautifully carved eighteenth-century desk.

'Remember this, Lee?' His voice was light, almost devoid of all emotion, but Lee's sensitive ears caught the faint note of triumph, her eyes fastening despairingly on the giveaway rose pink notepaper. It had been a present from her godmother on her sixteenth birthday. She had been thrilled with it at the time, but less than six weeks later the entire box had been consigned to the fire. —All but for two single sheets of the paper and one envelope.

'I wonder what that jealous fiancé of yours would have to say about this?' Gilles taunted. 'Even in to-day's more lax atmosphere, it still has a certain…something, would you not agree? Or perhaps you would care to refresh your memory?'

Lee shuddered deeply, averting her face, unable to even contemplate looking at the letter, never mind touching it.

'Alas, your modesty comes too late. Indeed, after reading this I doubt anyone would believe you ever possessed any. I read it again myself this morning, and while the vocabulary and style might leave a certain something to be desired, no one could fault the clarity of the sentiments. I believe I would be right in thinking that not even your beloved fiancé has a letter such as this to treasure from you…'

'Do you think I'd ever…' Lee burst out, goaded into answering. But Gilles stopped her.

'Perhaps not. Indeed I find it hard to equate the cool front you present to the world with the undeniable passion of this letter. Perhaps you would care for me to read you a passage or two, to refresh your mind…'

'No!' The word was a low moan, Lee's hands going up to cover her ears. She was shaking as though held deep in the grip of some fever, her eyes as dark as jade, and empty of everything but the agony she was experiencing.

'So,' Gilles murmured, apparently not in the slightest affected by her bowed shoulders and white face. 'It is agreed. Either you will marry me—temporarily—or I shall send a copy of this delightful love-letter to your fiancé. You have the night to think it over,' he added coolly. 'And, Lee, do not try to leave here, for that will surely guarantee your fiancé's sight of this charming epistle.'

Somehow she managed to get to her feet, to walk past Gilles on legs that trembled convulsively with every step. He stopped her at the door, his eyes raking her pale face without mercy.

'Strangely enough, you do have a certain air of breeding; a beauty that speaks of cloistered walls and untouched innocence. Be thankful that I know you for what you are and do not seek to take more from you than merely your time. Were you as cool and innocent as you appear, it would be…intriguing, awakening you to love.'

'To lust, don't you mean?' Lee said sharply in disgust. 'A man like you doesn't begin to know the meaning of the word love, Gilles.'

'Then we should make an excellent pair, shouldn't we?' he murmured insultingly as he held wide the door.

In her room Lee did not undress. She sat before the window, staring out into the moon-swept gardens, her eyes blinded by the tears cascading down her face as the present ceased to exist and she was once again that sixteen-year-old, trembling on the brink of life, and love.

It had all started as a joke. Aunt Caroline had a neighbour who had a daughter several months older than Lee, and when Lee stayed with her godmother, the two girls normally spent some time together.

With the benefit of hindsight, Lee wondered if Sally too had not had a crush on Gilles, just as she had done herself, but it was far too late now to query the whys and wherefores. The truth was that she had fallen deeply and intensely in love with Gilles, seeing him as a god to be worshipped adoringly from a distance, and Sally had discovered her secret and teased her with it.

That fatal day had been particularly hot. They had been lying in the uncut grass at the end of Aunt Caroline's long garden. Earlier Gilles had been cutting the lawn, muscles rippling under the smooth brown skin of his back, tanned in far sunnier climes than England's. Lee had watched him with her heart in her eyes. Soon he would be going back to France, his brief stay over, and she felt as though her heart would break.

As though she had read her mind, Sally had tempted as cunningly as Eve with her apple, 'I dare you to tell him how you feel.'

Lee had been horrified. She could think of nothing worse than that Gilles, so supercilious and unattainable, should know of her foolhardy impertinence.

'If you won't tell him, then I shall,' Sally had threatened with relish.

Lee had, of course, pleaded with her not to do—a foolish action, she now realised, and at length Sally had reluctantly agreed.

As she had claimed later, with a pert toss of her head, writing a letter was not telling, because she had not actually spoken to Gilles.

She had used her artistic talent to copy Lee's handwriting, and had signed the letter in Lee's name, using the very notepaper which Aunt Caroline had given Lee for her birthday. With so much evidence against her, it was small wonder that she had not been able to convince Gilles of her innocence, Lee reflected soberly, but his cruelty and callous disregard of how she had felt was something she would never forget.

Lee had been in her bedroom when Gilles found her. She had blushed the colour of a summer rose when he walked in. He looked so tall and handsome in his white shirt and tapering black trousers. The dark shadow of his tanned, muscular chest beneath the thin silk had triggered off an awareness of him she had not experienced previously, tiny tendrils of

fear-cum-excitement curling along her spine; the first
innocent awareness of sexual magnetism, but before
Gilles left her room the veil of innocence had been
torn aside for ever.

His presence in her room momentarily robbed her
of speech, but her heart had been in her eyes as she
looked up at him.

'Very appropriate,' he had sneered, his eyes on her
cross-legged pose on her bed, where she had been
doing some studying. 'But I regret, mademoiselle, I
have not come here to satisfy your nymphomaniac
desires, but to warn you of the outcome were you to
express the same sentiments to a man who is not honour bound to protect you from yourself.'

'I...'

'Save your breath,' he had warned her. 'These pru-
rient outpourings say it all.'

The letter had fluttered down from contemptuous
fingers to blur in front of the green eyes that read it
with growing disbelief. Some of the words, some of
the desires expressed were unfamiliar to her, but those
which she did understand were of such a nature as to
bring a flush of shame to her cheeks.

'Oh, but you can't think... I didn't write this!' she
had pleaded with him, but his face had remained
coldly blank.

'It is your handwriting, is it not?' he had demanded
imperiously. 'I have seen it on your schoolbooks—
schoolbooks! What would they say, those good nuns
who educate you, if they were to read this...this lewd
filth?'

'I didn't write it!' Lee protested yet again, but it was no use, he wouldn't even listen to her, and a schoolgirlish sense of honour prevented her from naming the real culprit. She felt as though she had suddenly slipped into some miry, foul pool, from whose taint she would never be clean again. The way Gilles was looking at her made her shudder with revulsion. She forgot that she had adored him, and felt only fear as she looked up into his condemning face.

'I have heard my friends talk of girls like you,' he had said at length, 'girls who use their lack of years to cloak their lack of innocence!' He spat out a word in French which she did not catch but was sure was grossly insulting, and then before she could move, reached for her across the brief intervening space and crushed her against his body, so that she was aware all at once of the vast difference between male and female, his hand going to her breast as his lips ground hers back against her teeth until she was crying with the pain, both her body and mind outraged by the assault.

'I hope you have learned your lesson,' he said in disgust when he let her go. 'Although somehow I doubt it. For girls like you the pain and degradation is a vital part of the pleasure, is this not so? Be thankful I do not tell Tante Caroline of this!'

Lee had practically collapsed when he had gone. Her mouth was cut and bleeding, her flesh scorched by the intimate contact with him, and although she had not understood a half of what she had read in the letter she was supposed to have sent, nor the insults he had heaped upon her head, she had set herself the task of learning—a long and arduous process when one's only source of knowledge was parents, the nuns, and gossip picked up from school friends whose practical knowledge was less than her own.

The incidents had had one salutary effect, though. It had killed for ever any desire for sexual experimentation; no other man was ever going to degrade her with insults such as those Gilles had hurled at her.

She came back to the present with a jerk as someone tapped faintly on her door. She frowned. If it was Gilles there was no way she could face a further attack upon her tonight.

'Lee, it's me.'

She sighed with relief as she heard Michael's brisk familiar tones. Her boss quirked an eyebrow in query as she opened the door.

'Well, have you been holding out on me, or was the announcement of the engagement as much a shock to you as it was to me?'

'You know I'm engaged to Drew.' She longed to be able to pour out her troubles to Michael, but his responsibility was to their employers, and his first charge was to secure the Chauvigny wine for their customers. At twenty-two she was old enough to sort out her own emotional problems, although quite how her present dilemma was to be resolved she had no idea.

'I take it it was all a plot to get rid of the clinging vine—Louise,' he elucidated when Lee looked blank. 'Neat piece of thinking.'

'Neater than you imagine,' she told him dryly. 'Gilles wants us to get married—strictly on a temporary basis, so that he can acquire some land from Louise's papa, without having to acquire Louise as part of the bargain.'

'And you being an old friend, he guessed that you would fall in with the idea,' Michael supplied, totally misunderstanding. 'Umm, well, I suppose it might work. Drew is likely to be tied up in Canada for twelve months, or so you told me when you applied for your job, and you shouldn't have any trouble getting the marriage annulled.'

Now, when it was too late, Lee wished she had told Michael the complete truth. But how did you tell a man that you were being blackmailed by a letter you had never written? In not challenging Gilles to do his worst, she had already tacitly admitted that Drew would believe she had written that letter, and why should Michael not do the same?

'In fact it could work out very nicely for us, altogether,' Michael commented, not entirely joking. 'As your husband Gilles would be sure to sell us his lesser quality wine. We've won the award for the best supermarket suppliers of wine for the last two years, and I'd like to make it three in a row, which would be almost definite if we get this wine.'

Her vague hope of appealing to Michael for some solution faded; he was, after all, first and foremost, a wine buyer, Lee reminded herself fairly, and as far as he knew what Gilles was proposing was merely an arrangement between friends.

'Well, Comtesse,' Michael commented with a grin, 'I'd better let you get some sleep. When's the wedding to be, by the way?'

'I haven't given Gilles my decision yet,' Lee protested lightly.

'Umm—well, I can't see him accepting it if it isn't in his favour,' Michael warned her. 'Your husband-to-be didn't strike me as a particularly persuadable man, my dear, so I should tread warily if I were you.'

Lee was already awake when dawn streaked the sky. She washed and dressed, then hurried downstairs. The house might have been deserted. In the courtyard where they had arrived she could hear the soft coo of doves. The clatter of horse's hooves over the drawbridge warned her that she no longer had the morning to herself, and she shrank back into the shadows as Gilles rode into the yard, astride a huge black stallion. Man and animal made an impressive picture, and Lee held her breath as they walked past her, unwilling to be found watching like a voyeur of two intensely male creatures.

The housekeeper stopped her in the hall, and Lee wondered how such a large woman managed to move so quietly, materialising almost as though by magic. '*Le petit déjeuner* will be served in the small salon,' she told Lee in repressive tones, her eyes sliding over the slim-fitting rose linen trousers Lee was wearing with a soft cream blouse and a matching rose linen sleeveless tunic.

It was on the tip of Lee's tongue to deny that she wanted anything to eat, but to do so would be an admission of defeat, and something in the house-keeper's eyes told her that the woman would dearly love to see her humiliated.

She paused by the stairs, her eyes drawn against her will to the portrait she had noticed before.

'René de Chauvigny,' Gilles commented quickly behind her, his hand on the banister over hers, pre-venting her flight. 'He was with Napoléon at the sack of Moscow and saved the Emperor's life. For that he was given these estates, which had belonged to his family before the Revolution, but which had passed into the hands of a second cousin who hated his ar-istocratic relatives enough to send them to the guil-lotine without compunction. The man you see por-trayed there was little better. He stole a young Russian girl away from her family, ravished her and then married her. The family legend has it that the Chauvigny betrothal ring was part of her dowry. So much did she hate her husband that she locked herself in one of the towers and refused to come out.'

Lee was appalled, contemplating the poor girl's fate. 'What happened to her?'

Gilles laughed mirthlessly. 'If you're comparing her fate with yours then don't. My foolish relative made the cardinal error of falling deeply in love with his captive bride, and the story goes that upon learn-ing that he loved her enough to send her back to her parents, the girl relented and came to love him in turn. What is more like it is that she discovered that lan-guishing alone in a tower can be dull and lonely, and decided to make the best of matters. Whatever the truth, she bore my ancestor three sons and two daughters.'

'She must have been very lonely and frightened.'

As she was frightened, Lee admitted, although not for the same reasons. How could she keep this temporary marriage a secret from Drew? She would have to tell him. If only she had told him about the letter, this would never have happened. But she had seen no reason—or perhaps suspected that he would not understand; that he too would condemn her for something for which she was not to blame. For the first time Lee wondered exactly how much value she put upon Drew's trust, if she was already doubting that it existed, and wasn't mutual trust, after all, a very important cornerstone for any marriage?

'Do not try to pretend that you are frightened,' Gilles taunted. 'Or is that why you hid from me in the shadows of the courtyard?'

So he had seen her! Lee turned, her eyes already darkening angrily, and found herself trapped against the banister, the warm, male smell of him invading her nostrils; his chest darkly shadowed beneath the thin silk shirt. She ought to have been repelled by such maleness. She preferred fair-haired men, men whose bodies were not so openly masculine, and yet some deeply buried nerve responded to the sight of his bared chest and long tanned throat in a way that made her lips part in soft dismay, her eyes clouding in disgust at her own reaction. Had Gilles been right after all? Was she the sort of woman who responded only to the savage maleness of men?

'Come, I have not yet had your answer; not yet heard from those sweet untouched lips that you will be my bride,' Gilles jeered. 'But then we both know that you will, don't we, Lee?'

'I don't have any choice in the matter. If I don't...'

'I will acquaint your fiancé with exactly what sort of female he is introducing to his correct Puritan family. Does he not care about all the men who have passed through your life, Lee, or is he so besotted that he has convinced himself that none of them matter?'

'Why should they?' Lee lashed back furiously. 'Not all men think it essential to find themselves an untouched virgin for a wife. Would you respect the academic whose chooses only to debate with those of inferior intellect? Or perhaps that's why men like virgins; it prevents women from discovering their shortcomings!'

'You wouldn't by any chance be issuing me a challenge, would you, Lee?' Gilles probed softly. 'Your body is very desirable—more desirable than I remember.' He studied her with insulting thoroughness; her soft breasts, outlined by the creamy fabric of her blouse; her narrow hips and long, slim legs. 'But no, I have no wish to be landed with you permanently, although any allegations you might make would hardly stand up in a court of law. Still, it might be as well were you to sign a document stipulating that this marriage will last only so long as I decree.'

His arrogance took Lee's breath away.

'You can't believe I would want to prolong it?' she

exclaimed bitterly. 'I can see no means of escaping from it, and much as it goes against the grain I shall have to agree, but make no mistake about it, Gilles. I'm not sixteen years old any longer. I'm not impressed by your chauvinistic machismo...'

'Marriage is a very intimate undertaking, and who is to say what you will and will not feel?'

'I love Drew, and I hate you. This farce of a marriage can't be over soon enough for me. And I should like my engagement ring back.'

'You shall have it—when our marriage is dissolved. For now, you will wear this.'

Lee gaped at the emerald ring he was sliding on to her finger. It was huge, glittering green fire through the darkness of the hallway, and as he slid it on to her finger Lee heard Gilles exclaim triumphantly, 'As I thought! It matches your eyes exactly. So, now we are betrothed.' And before Lee could stop him, his hands had left the banister to grasp the soft flesh of her upper arms, his dark head blotting out what little light there was as his lips grazed hers in a kiss which was more a stamp of possession than any tender gesture.

CHAPTER THREE

THEY were married three days later in Paris. Michael went with them and attended the brief ceremony. Lee knew it was irrational to feel so bereft of family and friends. After all, it was not a 'real' marriage. She could scarcely have asked her parents to be present, but it would have been nice to have Barbara and Pat there for moral support. The other two girls, in addition to being her flatmates, also worked for Westbury's, but in different departments, and the three of them got on exceptionally well. The Personnel Officer had suggested that Lee might like to share with them, when she explained that she had no accommodation in London. The previous member of the trio whom Lee was replacing had gone to work abroad, and the arrangement had worked out very well. She would have to write to them and let them know that it would be some time before she returned, and also to warn them about sending on her mail. They were good friends, but Lee couldn't help wondering what they would make of the situation. She could hardly not tell them about the marriage when Michael had witnessed it, but she could ask them to be discreet.

After the ceremony Gilles dismissed Michael with

promises to think carefully about supplying Westbury's with wine, and as Lee saw Michael's taxi disappearing towards the airport, she felt as though she
were saying goodbye to her last friend.

Why Gilles had chosen Paris for their marriage Lee
did not know, unless it was merely that he wished to
avoid the speculation of a local wedding, although
there was bound to be that, surely, when he returned
to the château with his bride?

They had been married in the morning, and now it
was afternoon and she was a wife of three hours, although Lee reflected that she doubted that she would
ever be able to think of Gilles as her husband. Her
enemy and tormentor perhaps; but her husband—
never!

They had a palatial suite of rooms in an exclusive
hotel, and when they returned there after the ceremony, Lee took the precaution of checking that the
communicating door between the bedrooms was
locked, before stepping out of the suit she had been
married in, and having a brief shower.

The blue linen suit was attractive enough, but it
was a far cry from the virginal white she had every
right—and desire—to wear, although of course she
would wear that for Drew. But somehow it wouldn't
feel the same; the ceremony would be besmirched by
the memory of today; of the curt words in French;
the touch of Gilles' hand as he guided hers in the
register before tears had blinded her when she tried
to write her name.

'Lee, open this door!'

The cold voice demanded admittance. She dressed hurriedly, staring at the locked door.

'Open it, Lee, or I shall ask the maid to come up with the pass-key.'

The threat decided her. She crossed the dove-grey carpet and unlocked the door. Gilles stood there, wearing the suit he had worn for the marriage ceremony, a soft, pale grey wool, impeccably tailored, and as he strode into her bedroom and removed the jacket, dropping it carelessly on her bed, she saw the name 'Pierre Cardin' stitched neatly inside.

'Couldn't you have worn anything better than that?' His eyes swept contemptuously over her suit.

Lee refused to feel threatened by the way he was prowling round her room, like a hungry panther waiting for his next meal.

'I didn't come prepared for a wedding.'

'You need new clothes.'

Lee stared at him resentfully.

'This afternoon we shall visit some of the couture houses and see if something can be organised.' Lee opened her mouth to protest, but was forestalled. 'As my wife you will have a position to maintain. After the vintage I entertain the buyers. As my wife and hostess you will be expected to mingle with women whose clothes and jewels come only from the finest houses.'

'The vintage?' Lee went white with dismay. 'But that's six months away!'

'So?' Gilles was very cool. 'Is six months of your life too high a price to pay for your fiancé's peace of mind, and my silence? By then Louise will have turned her attentions in other directions.'

'And you will be able to search for a dutiful, virginal bride in peace.'

Gilles inclined his head.

'You appear to take an inordinate amount of interest in the chastity of my eventual bride, but as she will be the mother of my children, it is only natural that I should wish her to be pure and untainted.'

'Unlike her husband.'

'Silence! You go too far! Do you goad me because I refuse to join you in the gutter? Be careful that I do not teach you the real meaning of degradation!'

NEVER HAD she seen so many breathtakingly elegant clothes, Lee thought in a daze. She and Gilles had been sitting on the dainty gilt chairs in this pale pink and dove grey salon for half an hour while model after model paraded in front of them, and so far Gilles had not said one word, apart from introducing Lee to the black-gowned vendeuse as his bride.

'My wife is young and has had a convent education,' he said at last, 'and I should like to see her dressed accordingly.'

The vendeuse's brow cleared instantly.

'We have an entire trousseau designed for a young South American girl, which is no longer required. An elopement, you understand, about which the family do not wish to talk. They are very proud and the girl had been reared from birth for the *grand mariage*.'

Lee's heart ached for the young South American,

and she mentally wished her happiness, as the vendeuse clapped her hands and spoke rapidly to the models.

'It is fortunate that your wife is so slim, although there may need to be alteration to the bustline…'

Lee flushed as Gilles' eyes rested contemplatively on the gentle thrust of her breasts.

'Indeed, my wife is undoubtedly female, for all her slimness of hip and thigh. Perhaps I may see some of the gowns on her.'

The vendeuse was all compliance, and Lee was bustled unwillingly to a changing room, where she was stripped of all but her briefs as yet another black-garbed woman assisted her into a thin cream wool dress, severely plain and yet somehow softly feminine, a river of tiny pleats cascading down one side to open in a soft fan when she walked.

Lee stared at herself in the mirror.

'It is perfect!' the vendeuse exclaimed. 'Indeed, Madame la Comtesse truly has an air of innocence and chastity which is emphasised by the gown. It is no wonder that Monseiur le Comte wishes the world to know of his wife's innocence.'

The world, or Louise? Lee wondered cynically, avoiding Gilles' eyes as she paraded dutifully in front of him.

'It is quite amazing what a difference clothes makes,' he commented sardonically, when she protested that she had enough clothes to last her a lifetime. 'Who seeing you in those gowns could disbelieve your virtue, and think that the clothes of a *fille de joie* would be more suited to your personality?'

'I'm surprised you didn't buy some for me,' Lee snapped, exhausted by the long hours of standing patiently being dressed and undressed like an animated doll. 'Just to remind me of exactly what I am, in case I get carried away by my new role!'

For a second something so cold and angry gleamed in his eyes that she wished the words unsaid.

'Perhaps I might at that,' he said softly, 'and then you can entertain me with all the tricks you have learned from your previous lovers.' He spoke quickly to the vendeuse, who was hovering several feet away, and after one dubious look at Lee the woman disappeared, to return with a dress that made Lee catch her breath in dismay.

It was jade green silk, exactly the same colour of her eyes, and she flinched as she was helped into it. She had always relished the thought of silk against her skin, but in this case it felt almost reptilian. The bodice was cut low over her breasts in the shape of waterlilies, each 'flower' moulding her flesh, the skirt slashed deeply up the front and edged with the same waterlily shape that floated round the hem. It was the dress of a woman who is either supremely sure of herself, or one who wants to make a definite statement of fact about her availability, and either way Lee hated it.

'It was designed for a television star,' the vendeuse explained, and Lee was not surprised. It had that sort of extravagant showiness about it.

She refused to look at Gilles when she modelled
it.

'We shall take it,' he told the modiste calmly, one
finger lightly tracing the outline of the silk against the
creamy flesh of Lee's breast. To the modiste that light
gesture would be the sort of embrace a new husband
might give to his bride, but Lee shivered uncontrol-
lably under it, knowing that it was Gilles' way of
showing his contempt for her body.

'It will serve to remind me that while for other men
my wife has the purity of the unattainable, for me,
she is...a woman.'

Lee flushed angrily. How dared Gilles do this to
her? The vendeuse was openly agog as she hurried
Lee back to the changing room. Did the woman interpret Gilles' words as a hint that he wanted his new
bride to himself all of a sudden? She almost laughed
at the falsity of it all.

Their shopping wasn't over. After the couturier's,
Gilles took her to an exclusive boutique smelling of
leather, where they bought shoes and handbags seem-
ingly for every occasion.

Lee's head was spinning when they emerged. What
on earth was Gilles going to do with all these clothes
when she left? Surely he wasn't contemplating giving
them to his real bride? The unrestrained laughter
building up inside her told her how close she was to
hysterics, and she swallowed hard on it, concentrating
instead on the lavish displays in the exclusive bou-
tiques they were passing. Ordinarily walking down
the Faubourg St Honoré would have been a treat all

on its own, but with Gilles at her side it was more of an ordeal.

'That should see you through for the time being,' he commented coolly, having hustled her in and out of an exclusive cosmetics house, where he had calmly instructed the gaping salesgirl to provide them with everything Lee would need to match the sophisticated glamour of the Frenchwomen with whom she would be mingling as Gilles' wife.

'Won't it rather jar the image of the innocent young bride?' she commented acidly at one point, watching the girl fill a small leather case with an assortment of eyeshadows and lipsticks.

'It will present an intriguing contrast,' Gilles told her without turning his head. 'The French are quick to pick up nuances, and they will not be slow to see behind the bride in her virginal clothes, experimenting with exotic make-up, the woman responding to the lessons of her lover.'

Lee felt sick. Everything Gilles did was designed purely to create an image which he himself believed to be false, merely to sustain his own pride of race. Of course it was unthinkable that a Chauvigny should marry a wanton, so because that was exactly what he believed her to be he had to create a mirage; a Lee whom he believed did not exist.

Lee was exhausted by the time they returned to the hotel. To her horror she discovered they were dining in their suite.

'It is expected,' Gilles told her casually. 'They know we were married this morning, and naturally no

Frenchman would want to spend his wedding night with other people.' He tossed a box towards her. 'You will wear this. Louise has many friends in Paris, most of whom will dine at least once a week at this hotel. I do not want them to hear gossip that the new Comtesse de Chauvigny dined with her new husband in blue linen,' he told her suavely.

'There's nothing wrong with my clothes,' Lee began hotly. 'They may not be expensive, but…' Her voice faltered into silence as she stared at the contents of the box. A nightgown and negligee in pure white silk poured through her fingers with fluid sensuality. The nightgown was completely plain, what there was of it. Lee swallowed as she saw the bias cut and realised how it would emphasise her body.

'I can't wear that!' she protested shakily. 'It's…I can't wear it, Gilles!'

'You can and will,' he told her equably, 'if I have to put in on you myself—an exercise neither of us would enjoy. It desecrates everything I believe in to see a woman like you wearing such a symbol of purity. Put it on,' he commanded curtly. 'Wear your hair down, and very little make-up. You have an hour.'

An hour to do what? Flee? Some hope! Gilles had her passport, and her money. She had woken up this morning to find them gone, and guessed by whose hand they had been removed from the handbag she had so carelessly left in the salon.

The white nightgown haunted her as she moved about the bedroom, delaying the moment when she must step into it.

She showered, rubbing her flesh briskly until it tingled, paling when she caught sight of her pale nudity in the mirrored walls. Her skin was the colour of cream where it had not even been touched by the sun, her breasts firm and taut. She moved her hands over them, her eyes suddenly very slumbrous as she tried to imagine how it would feel if she really were married and Drew was waiting for her on the other side of that communicating door. Her heart thumped painfully, her mouth dry, and she acknowledged bitterly that she would not have felt one thousandth of the dread she felt now.

As she had suspected the nightgown, so pure and virginal off, was anything but on. The silk caressed her skin, with soft, sinuous fingers, stroking over her breasts and outlining the nipples, falling into soft folds at her feet.

The negligee was little better. It was lined with silk as iridescent as mother-of-pearl, transferring a translucent gleam to her skin. Her eyes looked huge in her waxen face, her hair, a russet, silky waterfall on to her shoulders, shadowing her face as she bent forward to find the mules which had also been in the box. Deep bands of satin and lace cuffed the negligee and bordered the front. Every movement of her body was as fluid as water, Lee thought, watching her own reflection. It would be an enticement to any man to try to catch those fluid movements before they escaped him for ever, and she could only thank God that Gilles despised her sufficiently not to be the slightest bit stirred by her appearance.

He was waiting for her as she stepped into the salon, and the look he gave her made no allowances for her modesty. He was wearing a thin silk robe, monogrammed over the pocket. She supposed it was a dressing gown and shivered as she realised that under it he was naked—another part of this ridiculous charade.

'Come here!'

It never occurred to her to refuse. Her lips were dry with fear and tension and she touched them lightly with her tongue as he studied her.

'Perhaps I ought to give you that for your real wedding night,' he commented at last. 'Seeing you in it that poor besotted fiancé of yours could be forgiven for seeing only the angel in you.'

'But you, of course, know better.' For some reason his insistence on condemning her for something she did not do, his determination to see in her only what he wanted to see, was beginning to grate on Lee. 'What makes you think that he doesn't as well?' she demanded sweetly. 'It isn't exactly unknown for couples to anticipate their marriage vows, you know.'

'Bostonians share much in common with the French. He would never have suggested marriage if he thought he could get you any other way,' Gilles retorted crudely. 'No, you have deceived him with your mock innocence, but you cannot do so for ever, unless perhaps you intend to frequent one of those clinics that deal in human cynicism and for a considerable sum of money repair that which once having been torn, could never be rendered whole again.'

Lee went as white as her nightgown, her hand leaving a vivid imprint against Gilles' skin as she raised it to his face. Never in her life had she reacted so violently, and it shamed her to have done so now, but what he had been insinuating was insulting in the extreme.

'Why, you—!'

Strong fingers circled her wrist, uncaring of the fact that they were crushing fragile bones. She was held fast against Gilles and imprisoned by his arms, his hard body uncaring of her uncontrollable trembling.

'Had you really been my bride, you would not rest until you had done penance for that vicious action,' he told her through gritted teeth. 'No one strikes a Chauvigny without reprisal!'

Lee's heart beat frantically beneath the thin silk covering. She was unable to tear her eyes away from the livid fingermarks on the tanned cheek.

'You asked for it,' she said huskily, determined not to give way to the fear spiralling through her.

'And you asked for this!' Gilles grated back, his mouth fastening on hers, as though he intended to drain her completely of the will to defy him ever again. Her heart almost stopped beating, and then started again, at twice its previous rate. She tried to move her head, but Gilles' fingers grasped her hair, pulling it hard until her throat was arched back vulnerably, her lips crushed beneath his as he reinforced the lesson he seemed determined she must learn. His free arm had been clamped about her waist, holding her against the taut maleness concealed only by the thin silk, but as Lee tried to pull away his hand moved upwards pushing aside the negligee to fasten determinedly on the soft fullness of one breast, the nightgown ruthlessly removed to allow his fingers freer access to her flesh; to allow his thumb to circle her nipple slowly and spark off sensations which made her cringe in self-disgust. Reaction shuddered through her. Gilles' hand left her breast to tilt her face up to meet the smoky investigation of his eyes.

'You must have been a long time without a lover,' he taunted softly. 'What is it your body pleads for, Lee? This?' His hand returned to her breast, shaking her with the depth of response the single embrace culled from her. 'Or this?' His head bent, dark against the creamy softness of her flesh and her moan of mingled pain and pleasure was clearly heard as his lips took the place of his hand, sending shuddering waves of emotion washing through her. No one had touched her like this. No one had shown himself to be so completely the master of her body, of its innermost secrets and desires. Feelings she had never dreamed could exist rose up inside her to mock her earlier defiance as her flesh melted to his touch. He raised his head, and for a moment Lee thought she saw the devil himself in his eyes, and yet still her overwhelming longing was to drag the dark head back to her now aching breasts, to push aside that thin silk robe and taste the tangy male flesh.

'Or this?' Gilles said softly, lifting her in his arms and carrying her through the salon, to the rich masculinity of his own bedroom. She had not been in it before, but noticed nothing but the heavy mahogany furniture and the shadowy outline of the huge bed.

Some last remnants of sanity urged her to protest, but this was quickly stifled beneath Gilles' impatient hands as he lowered her on to the bed and deftly removed the slender wisp of silk.

Her heartbeat sounded as loud as thunder, and she turned her head, unable to bear Gilles' close scrutiny. His hands cupped her face, forcing her to meet his eyes.

'You're letting the past swamp the real you,' he goaded softly. 'I'm not the first man to look upon you like this by any means, Lee, although I suspect you have seldom looked so cool and virginal; even the first time.'

Despite the cruel words his voice held a seductive quality that lulled her fears, like a panther lulling its prey into a false sense of security.

'Did you know, that summer, I actually contemplated sleeping with you myself? You were so fresh and innocent, or so I thought. I told myself I could not be the one to so carelessly pluck such a rare flower, still only in the bud, but someone else had been before me, hadn't they, my oh, so experienced little wife? The bud is already rotten!'

Lee couldn't answer. There was a huge lump in her throat. Gilles, subduing his desires because of her innocence. Had it really been like that? Of course not. How could it have been?

His hands on her body drew a broken protest past her lips. It was silenced with a kiss, so sweet and

tender that Lee felt her whole body melt into heated
warmth, her arms lifting towards him, but they were
held, pinioned above her head, while Gilles began a
thorough arousal of her body, the kisses he stroked
against her now ardent flesh punctuated by soft murmuring enquiries as to whether she was enjoying his
unhurried touch. Her body gave him the answer, and
shame made her eyes smart with tears as she contemplated her own complete inability to control its betraying reactions. She longed to reach up and part
Gilles' robe, to feel his hard male warmth against her,
and yet the very strength of her longing shocked and
appalled her. She had never felt like this with Drew—
but then Drew had never held her like this, his lips
moving from one rosy-peaked breast to the other, and
then on downwards, until her stomach muscles con-
tracted in virginal protest at the path taken by those
questing lips.

At last her arms were released, but something about
the look in Gilles' eyes forestalled her immediate reaction, which was to reach up for him. They were
cold, as cold and bitter as the North Sea, and already
she was shivering under their impact.

'Perhaps in future you'll think twice before raising
your hand to me again,' he said coolly, sliding off the
bed. 'We both know you wanted to provoke me into
taking you, to appease your own insatiable appetites,
but I think this is a more fitting punishment, don't
you?' He smiled cruelly into her aroused features.
'Much more fitting. For a woman of your experience
you were a little too trusting, my dear, or did you

think the sight of that sexy little body would make me forget what it conceals? Now get out of my room!'

He was reaching for the phone as he issued the curt command. Shivering with self-disgust, Lee gathered up her nightdress, trying to control the pain he had just caused her. He had quite deliberately aroused her, just so that he could throw these taunts at her, she knew that now. But it wouldn't happen again.

'If you're ordering dinner, I don't want any,' she told him bitterly. 'I'm not hungry.'

'Liar,' he said succinctly, turning to glance down the length of her still nude body. 'But I wasn't. I want to get someone up here to change the bed. I detest sleeping in soiled sheets.'

Lee went white, swaying slightly as she turned towards the door. Never in her life had she been subject to such humiliation, and for one brief second she contemplated challenging him with the proof that all his accusations were unjust. But what was the use? He would probably take her with the same callous arrogance with which he had aroused her, and then mock her for allowing him the intimacies only Drew should have been permitted.

Somehow she managed to stagger back to her room. In the sitting room was mute evidence that their meal had arrived and had been left discreetly on a heated trolley. No doubt their non-appearance for dinner was perfectly acceptable in a newly married couple, but the smell of the food nauseated Lee as she turned aside and walked blindly into her own room.

Once there she stripped off the negligee she had covered herself with, and stood in the shower, with the water beating angrily into her flesh, but when she emerged from it she still did not feel clean. The marks of Gilles' fingers stood out clearly on her breasts, which seemed to her critical and sickened eyes to be fuller, tauter than before. She retched suddenly, heaving on an empty stomach as sickness swept her. She was loathsome, depraved. She had allowed Gilles to treat her as the woman he had accused her of being; she had actually responded to his vile, calculated caresses; she had actually *wanted* them, and that was something which no amount of water could wash away.

There were no tears; she was beyond that. Gilles was right—tonight she had learned a lesson she would never forget. It was branded into her flesh and burned into her soul.

If there was any way she could have left him she would have taken it. Only twice in her life had she tasted the hell men and women make for one another, and both times it was Gilles who had taken her there. There must never be a third time; because if there was she doubted that she had the ability to return. Already the horror of what had happened threatened to overwhelm her normal common sense. Her eyes strayed to the phone and she was convulsed with a longing to hear Drew's gentle voice, to beg him to take her away from Gilles—but if she did that he would want to know why, and she could not tell him. She had betrayed his trust; she had let another man

gain intimate knowledge of her, so how could she go
to Drew now and plead his aid?

During the night something woke her. Her face and
pillow were damp with tears, and as she lay, testing
the darkness of the unfamiliar room, it came to her
that the sound which had awoken her had been her
own crying. She had not cried like that since... Since
the summer she was sixteen.

CHAPTER FOUR

THEY didn't linger in Paris, but then why should they? Lee thought listlessly, watching Gilles place her brand new suitcases containing the clothes he had bought her in the boot of his gleaming silver-green Mercedes sports car; after all, they were not real honeymooners.

Remembering the degrading events of the previous evening, she shuddered deeply and found Gilles' grey eyes resting on her pale face with grim appraisal. When he closed the boot he came across to her, his fingers forcing her chin upwards so that he could study her more closely.

'A little pallor in a bride is acceptable,' he said coldly, 'but you look as though you've spent the night in a house haunted by ghosts. To everyone else this marriage is a very real one, Lee, and if you give them the slightest cause to doubt that, I shall know how to punish you.'

'How, by inflicting your repulsive presence on me?'

Instead of being annoyed he merely laughed, a soft taunting sound that set her nerves on edge.

'Oh, I'm sure I can think of something. I managed all right last night.'

Lee wrenched her chin out of his hand, her fierce, 'Don't remind me of that!' drawing his brows together in a dark frown.

'You are not required to act the part of the affronted virgin, Lee, and I have already told you this. If, by adopting this pose, you are hoping to convince me that you felt no frustration, no longing for fulfilment last night, then don't. Your body gave you away most obviously.'

Lee couldn't reply for the sudden rush of tears which threatened to blind her. Like a sleepwalker she moved towards the car, dimly conscious of Gilles climbing in beside her, but when he reached across her to secure her seat belt she thrust him aside, her fingers trembling over the stiff mechanism, her bitter, 'Don't touch me!' lost in the powerful roar of the Mercedes' engine as they pulled away from the kerb.

The route was now vaguely familiar, but she was startled when they stopped just outside Blois, and Gilles negotiated the Mercedes down an unmade, rutted road to a small manor house set amidst a walled vineyard.

They hadn't exchanged so much as a word during the journey, and pride prevented Lee from speaking now. They drove into a cobbled courtyard, far less impressive than that belonging to the château, and a sturdy dark-haired man of Gilles' age emerged from the manor house, a beaming smile splitting his tanned face as he saw the Mercedes.

'Gilles!'

The two men embraced fondly, and then Gilles

turned to Lee. 'Jean-Paul, I should like you to meet my wife, Lee, the new Comtesse de Chauvigny.'

For a moment the man Jean-Paul merely stared at Lee, and then he said something rapidly to Gilles in French, accompanied by a wide grin. Lee longed to ask what was going on, but Jean-Paul was opening the car door for her, and a glance at Gilles showed that he too was climbing out of the car.

'*Un moment*, I must tell Marie-Thérèse of your arrival. You will eat with us, of course?'

He had switched back to English, for her sake, Lee suspected. She did speak a little French, but unless it was spoken very slowly she found the language hard to follow.

'Why else do you think we stopped?' Gilles joked, suddenly looking much younger than Lee could have believed possible.

Jean-Paul disappeared towards the house.

'Jean-Paul and Marie-Thérèse are old friends of mine,' Gilles explained, grasping Lee's arm to prevent her from escaping. The movement brought her into close contact with his thigh, her body cringing immediately as she forced herself to remember last night's humiliation. Gilles appeared not to notice her distress. His eyes were fixed on the open door of the small manor house.

'Jean-Paul inherited the Clos des Fleurons from his uncle several years ago and since then he has worked hard to bring it up to scratch. His uncle bought it as a hobby and the vines had been badly neglected. This year Jean-Paul is hoping to gain an Appellation Contrôlée designation.'

Lee was duly impressed. Gilles' wine already carried this seal of approval, and as she knew, only seventeen per cent of the wine produced in France in any one year was permitted the coveted accolade.

They had only covered a few yards of the distance to the door, when a young woman hurried through it, her dark hair caught up in an elegant chignon, her entire appearance neatly elegant despite the fact that she was in the later stages of pregnancy.

Lee watched as Gilles kissed her affectionately, laughing as he complained that he could no longer get near to her.

'Just you wait, Gilles!' Marie-Thérèse threatened lightly, glancing towards Lee, who had automatically moved aside to allow Gilles to greet his friend's wife. 'Soon it will be your turn, *non*?'

Lee flushed scarlet as Marie-Thérèse's eyes studied her slender frame, shuddering as Gilles' hand descended to her shoulder, grasping it meaningfully.

'Lee is still very much a new bride, Marie-Thérèse,' he said in a low voice, enriched with sensual appeal, as though he was reminding his friends that his wedding night was not long past, and still held cherished memories. 'You embarrass her by suggesting that she might already be carrying my child. Is this not so, *petite*?'

Lee glared furiously at him, tempted to remind him in front of his friends exactly what had happened last night, but as though he sensed the direction of her thoughts, his fingers bit into the tender skin of her shoulder, his eyes like iron as they warned her of the punishment any defiance would warrant.

'We are unkind to tease you,' Marie-Thérèse apologised. 'Please come with us. You will want to freshen up before lunch.'

As Lee followed her into a huge, old-fashioned kitchen, fragrant with herbs and the delicious smell of cooking food, Marie-Thérèse added, 'We were so surprised when Gilles telephoned us from Paris this morning to say that he was married. For a moment we feared the worst, that Louise had trapped him at last.' She paused by a doorway which led to a narrow flight of stairs, her expression concerned as she saw Lee's pale face. 'Forgive me! Perhaps you did not know about Louise…'

'I did know,' Lee assured her with a brief smile. In other circumstances she could have enjoyed the French girl's company. She was about Lee's own age, and grimaced ruefully over the old-fashioned bathroom to which she escorted Lee.

'It is old-fashioned is it not? Oncle Henri neglected the property and for now we must concentrate on the vines. Perhaps later there will be money to spare for the house.'

'I am sure you will find a difference once Jean-Paul has been awarded the Appellation Contrôlée,' Lee comforted her. 'Gilles was just telling me how hard you had worked.'

'I no longer,' Marie-Thérèse murmured. 'Now that I am *enceinte* Jean-Paul does not permit me to work in the fields. You will soon discover that to a *vigneron* his vines are a mistress who will rival his wife all their lives. Have you known Gilles long?'

She supposed she ought to have been prepared for that question, Lee thought. It was plain that Marie-Thérèse was very fond of Gilles.

'Sort of,' she temporised, unwilling to unleash Gilles' anger upon her hapless head by saying the wrong thing. 'My godmother is Gilles' aunt, and I knew him as a child.'

'And he, seeing the beautiful woman you would one day become, has waited all these years for you! It is *très romantique*!'

Lee did not bother to disillusion her. The manor house, in direct contrast to the château, was shabby, furnished sparsely, but it did at least have the advantage of being reasonably large, Marie-Thérèse commented as she showed Lee over it. The two men were sitting in the kitchen, drinking wine from the plain glasses connoisseurs always use. 'They will talk for hours if we let them,' Marie-Thérèse complained. 'Gilles has been very good to us. It is he who has persuaded the Institut National des Appellations d'Origine to consider us. This is something he is under no obligation to do, and we are very grateful to him. But come, unless we return to the kitchen the lunch which I have prepared to celebrate your marriage will be quite ruined.'

Lee was grateful that her knowledge of French eating habits had prepared her for what was to come.

The lunch was delicious and lasted for two hours,

comprising four courses, excluding the cheese. When the hors-d'oeuvres had been cleared away and the delicious lobster eaten, Marie-Thérèse served them with a chicken casserole cooked in Jean-Paul's own wine. It was delicious, and when Lee had eaten every scrap Marie-Thérèse commented wickedly to Gilles,

'Now, my friend, you will not look so smug. I have put in Lee's chicken herbs to make her fruitful, and soon too she will look like me, *non*?'

They all laughed, even Lee, who did not want to upset or hurt Marie-Thérèse, but still she could not help blushing, and Gilles who had been watching her remarked suavely,

'Excellent though your herbs may be, Marie-Thérèse, they alone will not have the desired effect, is that not so, *chérie*?'

Lee was glad of the general laughter. It prevented her from having to reply, and even though she had enjoyed the company of the young couple, she was glad when they eventually departed. Keeping up the façade of a deliriously happy bride was taxing every last bit of her mental reserves, and as Jean-Paul kissed her enthusiastically on both cheeks, she wondered anew just how she was going to endure the next six months.

The afternoon was warm, with the sun shining down hotly, and when Gilles suggested removing the hood of the Mercedes, Lee did not object.

The cool air, tugging teasingly through her hair, the warm, burgeoning smell of growing things, the blue vastness of the sky above them all helped to relax her taut nerves, and as they drove through Tours, the sleep which had eluded her all through the previous night finally embraced her, her breathing light and even as her eyelids fluttered closed.

When she awoke they were in the courtyard of the château, and Gilles' wolfhound was bounding towards the car. Still half asleep, Lee struggled to sit up, appalled to discover that she had been leaning on Gilles' shoulder, and that his arms were at that very moment intent on making her a prisoner.

As he kissed her she could taste the wine on his mouth, and the familiarity, instead of being repellent, sent waves of awareness flooding over her. The sun was shining directly into her eyes, so she closed them, lying passively in Gilles' arms, too drugged with sleep and sunshine to move.

At last he released her.

'Now you are beginning to learn. No one observing our arrival can have doubted that we are indeed truly man and wife.'

Before she could speak he was out of the car, opening her door, and bending to take her weight.

To the astounded housekeeper who met them at the door he said calmly, 'This is an English custom. Have my orders been followed?'

Without waiting for a reply he strode towards the stairs, mounting them easily, despite the burden of her weight, Lee noted drowsily. Through his shirt she could see the darkness of his hair-roughened chest, and a feeling so intensely alien that it shocked her surged up through her veins. For one moment she had actually wanted to stretch out and touch her husband, to discover exactly how that alien maleness felt beneath her fingers. Green eyes mirrored her appalled shock, her hands immediately clenching into two small fists as though to prevent any further traitorous impulses. In fact she was so intent on quelling the unfamiliar surge of feeling which had stolen over her that at first Lee was unaware of the import of the huge double bed Gilles had dropped her on to, or the fact that she had been brought to a different room from that she had occupied before.

It was Gilles, removing his shirt and discarding it carelessly to disappear into an en suite bathroom who alerted her to the truth, her sun-blinded eyes beginning to observe things she had not noticed before, such as the grandeur of the bedroom, the elegance of the beautiful antiques with which it was furnished, the careless way in which Gilles returned to spatter droplets of water on to the priceless Aubusson carpet, his torso gleaming like polished silk as he opened another door and disappeared into what Lee guessed must be a dressing room, to return with a clean shirt, his expression sardonic as he looked into her startled eyes.

'What's the matter? Don't you care for the bridal suite?'

The bridal suite! She had known all along, of course, but it had taken Gilles' callous words to crystallise all her fears. She stared at the bed, moistening her dry lips with the tip of her tongue as she lifted wary eyes to his face.

'You can't mean...' She swallowed nervously, forcing herself to go on. 'You can't mean that we have to share this room, Gilles?'

'Of a surety I do. And not only the room, but the bed as well. The men who work for me are earthy French peasants. How long do you suppose I will continue to merit their respect once it becomes known that I sleep apart from my wife? Or were you hoping that separate bedrooms would give you the opportunity to indulge your carnal appetites elsewhere? Think of yourself as doing a penance, Lee,' he mocked. 'And how much sweeter the wine of love will taste after six months' abstinence; although I suppose that is like promising a rare wine to an alcoholic. To him the quality matters little, is this not so? It is the quantity that counts.'

Lee scrambled off the bed, her face white with shocked distaste.

'Marriage to you doesn't give you the right to talk to me like...'

'Like a woman of the streets?' Gilles taunted. 'She at least is honest in what she offers, Lee. In a moment they will be bringing up the cases. If at any time during the next six months you give anyone the impression that our marriage is not filled with bliss and happiness, I shall exact a penalty from you that you will never, ever forget.'

From somewhere Lee found the courage to say curtly, 'Obviously you don't hold to the theory that the donkey might respond better to the carrot than the stick!'

For a moment his eyes seemed to burn into her, and then in a voice that made her feel as brittle as fine-blown crystal he said softly.

'And precisely what "carrot" did you have in mind, Lee? Or can I guess? Your good behaviour in return for my satisfaction of those desires you have such difficult in controlling?' He laughed harshly. 'Haven't I already told you that I don't like soiled goods?'

The arrival of a swarthy man carrying her cases prevented her from replying. The housekeeper was hard on his heels, her eyes malicious and curious as she stared from Lee to Gilles.

'Perhaps when she has time Madame might care for me to show her over the château, and there is also the matter of the dinner Monsieur le Comte was planning for next week...' She let her voice fade away, hinting more at Lee's inability to cope with such a responsibility rather than Gilles' reluctance to go through with it in view of his newly married state.

'Some other members of our local wine-growing commune,' Gilles explained coolly. 'I had intended to talk with them about their views on this year's harvest.'

'Madam Louise has acted as Monsieur's hostess in the past,' the housekeeper interrupted in tones which acquainted Lee with the reason for the woman's hostility. It was plain that the housekeeper considered Louise a far better person to be the new Comtesse than Lee herself.

Half to her own surprise Lee heard herself saying

coolly, 'I am sure we shall be able to manage. And then of course there will be the vintage, and the buyers' dinners to arrange. I take it the buyers normally stay overnight?'

Gilles nodded. An idea was beginning to take shape in Lee's mind. She knew all about these dinners and she had it in mind to wipe the supercilious look from the faces of Gilles and his housekeeper, by showing them what an English hostess could do when she set her mind to it.

'I shall be ready to look over the château when I have changed,' Lee told the housekeeper. The woman was already looking faintly taken aback by Lee's refusal to be put off by her cold manner, and Lee decided that now was as good a time as any to reinforce the fact that she was now mistress of the château, no matter on how temporary a basis. Immaculate and elegant the house might be, but it lacked those little touches that made it a home; nowhere had she seen any flowers, for instance; nowhere had she sensed that warmth that comes from a house filled with love and laughter—but then of course she was hardly likely to find *that*.

'We should like some coffee,' she told the housekeeper calmly. 'Gilles, do you want something to eat?'

If her 'husband' was surprised at this sudden show of wifely concern he did not betray it.

'Coffee will be fine.'

Lee saw the housekeeper's mouth tighten as she obeyed the command, and knew that this was but the first battle in what threatened to be a hard-fought campaign.

When she had gone, Gilles asked Lee curtly, 'What was all that about?'

'I'm surprised a man of your perception needs to ask,' Lee replied dryly. 'Surely it can't have escaped your notice that she would have preferred you to marry Louise?'

'I hadn't thought about it, although come to think of it, Louise did recommend her to me. She has always fulfilled her duties properly.'

'I'm sure she has,' Lee agreed. 'If you wish her to continue to run this house, Gilles, then please say so, it makes no difference to me, although I suspect that had you actually married the shy young bride you seemed determined to have, Madam Le Bon would have lost no time in putting her very firmly in her place.'

She turned away, busying herself with the contents of the first suitcase, but she was aware of Gilles watching her thoughtfully, and when she marched towards the dressing room carrying an armful of clothes he said slowly,

'You are now the mistress of this château, but I warn you, Lee, if it is not run as efficiently as it has been in the past, I shall have no compunction in giving Madam Le Bon the right to run it once more!'

She had been warned, Lee thought half an hour later, grimacing over the half cold coffee which a blushing young girl had just brought into the bedroom. She had changed into her own linen suit, and

was alone in the room, Gilles having complained that
he had no intentions of waiting all afternoon for a cup
of coffee when he had work waiting for him. She had
heard him call to his dog as he left the house, and
from the clatter of horses's hooves across the courtyard guessed that he had ridden out to inspect the
vines.

When she joined the housekeeper for her tour of
inspection she made no comment on the coffee.

The château was larger than she had first realised,
built foursquare round the enclosed courtyard, one
wing given over entirely to stables, garages and stor-
age rooms.

Of the other three, one contained a huge ballroom,
which Lee did not need to be told was almost an exact
replica of the Galerie des Glaces at Versailles although on a somewhat smaller scale. The room
needed painting, and from the grime on the windows
had obviously not been used for a very long time.

'Every Chauvigny bridegroom has given a ball for
his new bride in this room,' the housekeeper told her
sourly, and Lee knew she meant to underline the fact
that Gilles had made no such suggestion to *his* bride's
case. Lee ignored her. She had her own plans for the
ballroom, which had only come to her as she realised
exactly how suitable it would be for what she had in
mind.

'It needs cleaning and painting,' was her only comment, but even this was not allowed to go unremarked
as the housekeeper objected acidly, 'Only Monsieur
le Comte has the authority to give such orders.'

Lee lost count of the number of bedrooms the château possessed. Many were closed up, their furniture under covers, and as the housekeeper showed her the rooms in the South Tower which had once belonged to the Russian girl who had been stolen away by Napoleon's Captain, Lee expelled her breath on a delighted sigh.

The rooms were cold, and only small; there was a bedroom, the walls hung with pale green silk, a comfortable window seat covered in the same material, the bed enclosed with shimmering green silk draperies suspended from a gold circlet set in the ceiling. It was a girl's room rather than a woman's, as fresh and innocent as its owner had been before her ravisher stole her away from the safety of her family. And yet she had come to love him. For some reason Lee felt herself trembling deeply inside.

The sitting room on the floor below, connected to the bedroom with its own spiral staircase, was equally enchanting, decorated in the same soft green as the bedroom, but this time with touches of palest pink, in the Aubusson carpet, and the brocade-covered chairs. It was easy to imagine the Russian girl here, dreaming perhaps of her home, alone and forlorn, until her rebellious heart betrayed her to the man who had brought her to this silken prison.

'I shall use this room as my office,' Lee told Madam Le Bon. The woman looked less than pleased, and muttered something Lee could not catch, as she preceded her back into the main part of the house.

The kitchens were last on the agenda; huge cav-

ernous rooms looking out on to the courtyard, fragrant
as only a French kitchen can be. The cook was a
middle-aged woman, dressed in black, her hair
screwed up into a bun, busily commanding several
giggling maids until Lee's arrival interrupted her, and
Lee sensed that while the woman might be reserving
judgment, she had not taken an immediate dislike to
her as the housekeeper had.

'We shall need to talk about the menus for Monsieur le Comte's guests,' Lee told her, ignoring the
housekeeper's disapproval. 'And perhaps some way
of ensuring that the coffee is hot when it reaches our
bedroom.'

The housekeeper frowned and darted a bitter look
at Lee. The cook started to say something, breaking
off when Lee shook her head to indicate that she was
going too fast. When she spoke more slowly Lee
could understand. The housekeeper had said nothing
of any coffee to her, and of course Madam could have
hot coffee. She would see to it herself.

They parted on amicable terms, Lee heaving a
slight sigh of relief. She suspected that the cold coffee
had been a deliberate attempt to make her look small
on the part of the housekeeper, who had probably
thought that in the interest of good relations she
would not complain. Lee knew the French better than
that. They would not have any respect for anyone who
accepted inferior food or drink, no matter how simple
it might be.

Back in her own room Lee stripped off her suit and
headed for the bathroom. Many of the rooms had been

dusty, and she could not change into one of her new dresses without first having at least a shower.

The bathroom was equipped with both shower and bath of such a luxurious quality that Lee caught her breath. Gilles certainly didn't stint himself on any of his creature comforts, she thought, remembering Marie-Thérèse's old-fashioned plumbing.

With the shower turned on, Lee didn't hear Gilles enter the bedroom, and her first intimation that he had returned came only when she stepped out of the shower and found him watching her in a manner that made the hot colour run up under her skin, as she stretched out a trembling hand for the towel she had placed in readiness on the small stool.

Gilles was quicker.

'Why shouldn't I look at my wife if I want to?' he mocked when she started to protest. 'I'm surprised at you, my dear. Watching you shower was quite an education. You do not touch yourself like a woman who knows the full power of her own sexuality—or perhaps you don't bother when you don't have an audience.'

Lee forgot her nudity long enough to say shakily, 'That's a disgusting thing to suggest! I...'

She shivered suddenly, drops of moisture sparkling against her skin. Gilles' eyes darkened and for a moment she almost held her breath, quivering under the burning intensity of his gaze. She took a step forward to re-claim her towel, and with a sudden groan Gilles hauled her into his arms, uncaring that her damp body was pressed against his clothes, his breath rasping slightly as it left his lungs.

He smelled of the open air, horses, and clean sweat, and Lee trembled with the sudden realisation that she found the combination erotic, for otherwise why would her body feel as though it had been invaded by alien emotions?

'You're a witch! Do you know that?' Gilles muttered huskily against her skin. 'Even knowing what you are, I still desire you, but that's what you wanted, isn't it, Lee? That's why I found you waiting for me so enticingly… God, why not?' she heard him groan hoarsely 'I'm a man, after all, not a plaster saint, and when your appetite's been sharpened like mine, even the toughest meat tastes like ambrosia!'

His breath was hot against her skin, his eyes glazed with a desire that struck terror into Lee's heart. She tried to pull away, but her frantic movements only seemed to excite him further. The kiss that punished her defiance sapped both her strength and her will. She could feel the tautly male outline of him against her body, and trembled in mingled fear and resentment.

It was only the second knock on their bedroom door that brought his head up, anger tightening his mouth as Madame Le Bon entered without permission His bulk hid Lee's nakedness from the other woman, although whether this was by accident or design Lee did not know.

'Will you wish dinner at the usual time, madame?' she asked Lee expressionlessly. Lee had already informed her that for now they would continue with the normal routine and she suspected the woman had deliberately waited until now, hoping to interrupt a tender moment and distress the new bride. After she had shown Lee the kitchens she had taken her down to the cellars. Since childhood Lee had had a fear of being locked in a dark room, and she had sensed the woman watching her with malicious amusement as she had given them only the most cursory inspection.

To Lee's surprise, before she could answer the housekeeper's question, Gilles had swung open the bedroom door.

'I suggest if you wish to retain your position here, madame, you exercise a little more discretion,' he told her curtly. 'We are, after all, a very newly married couple!'

Bright patches of colour stained the housekeeper's cheeks, and Lee found herself holding her breath as she stalked out of the room. She had half expected Gilles to enjoy her own humiliation of being discovered practically on the point of being made love to by him, but perhaps he considered reprimanding the housekeeper's insolence more important than mocking her embarrassment.

Whatever the truth, the moment Madame Le Bon was gone Gilles released Lee, grimacing in self-disgust.

'Perhaps I should not have been so hard on Madame Le Bon,' he said cruelly. 'Had she not arrived when she did I might have given myself true reason to feel self-loathing—something you will know nothing about,' he jeered.

If only he knew! This was the second time she had been held in his arms and felt the beginnings of those emotions which seemed to rob her of her willpower. Emotions to which she was a stranger, but which she knew instinctively were dangerous when connected with her position here as Gilles' wife—a wife he had made no secret of despising for her supposedly amoral conduct.

They dined in silence, and afterwards Gilles stood up and announced that he was going to his office.

Left to her own devices, Lee went into the library and selected a book to read. Her eye was caught by a history of the Chauvigny family and she took it down from the shelves. It was dusty—another sign of the housekeeper's neglect. Tomorrow she would draw up a plan of action, Lee decided. It didn't matter that the groundwork she did now would ultimately benefit Gilles' real wife, at all costs she must keep busy during the enforced six months of her imprisonment. She would also have to write to Drew. She had decided to tell him that she was working at the château; other explanations would have to await their reunion, and she had enough problems without dwelling on those yet to be faced.

Reading the history was a laborious process, but an interesting one. She read that the château had been built during the time of François I, by a Chauvigny who had been close to the pleasure-loving monarch, but who had eventually been banished from court for seducing a young lady François himself had had his eye on. That Henri de Chauvigny had later married the girl had apparently not softened François' heart towards him, and that incident was but one example of the Chauvignys' chequered history—a history closely intertwined with that of France itself, and clearly showing the sensual greed of the Chauvigny males, Lee thought distastefully.

At eleven o'clock she closed the book and went upstairs. This moment had been at the back of her mind since she first realised that she and Gilles were to share a room. That he intended this purely as an additional unpleasantness for her Lee already knew, and so it was, but not in the way that Gilles envisaged. He thought she would be tormented by his un-attainable presence in bed beside her; Lee's all-consuming fear was that the desire she had already glimpsed once in his eyes might flare up again and totally destroy her.

The bedroom was empty. Lee switched on the light, and this time carefully securing the bathroom door, prepared for bed. She did not emerge from the bathroom until she was dressed in her nightgown and the thin silk robe that had been part of the trousseau Gilles had bought for her.

SHE NEED NOT have bothered. There was no sign of Gilles. The satin sheets felt cold and hostile and as she slid between them Lee found herself longing for the familiar comfort of her narrow single bed, at home in London. As she lay there unhappy tears slid from her eyes as she contemplated how life might have been if she had not had the misfortune to encounter Gilles. Already he had cost her the job she loved, much of her self-respect, and innumerable heart-searchings, how much more pain was there to be before she was set free?

She didn't hear him come to bed, and when she awoke in the morning he was gone, and this set the pattern for their days. One of the maids brought her breakfast in bed. It seemed that the cook thought a newly married woman needed to build up her strength before rising from her bed in the morning, and Lee enjoyed the sensual pleasure of lying in her bed, watching the sun stroke the vines in tender caress as she ate freshly baked croissants and drank the reviving hot coffee. In fact Lee was beginning to discover many things about herself there had never been time to learn before; some of them pleasant, some of them not so pleasant, and among those that weren't was her growing awareness of Gilles as a man.

She had taken to avoiding being in their room when he arrived back from the fields late in the afternoon. There was something about the earthy scent of his flesh, the beginnings of a beard along his jaw, the exposed skin of his chest, which was opening her mind and senses to emotions she had not previously known existed. It was as though the intimacy of marriage was acting like a hothouse atmosphere, forcing into life those emotions which had been shocked into hibernation all those many years ago.

During dinner one night the phone rang. Gilles
went to answer it and came back frowning.

'That was Louise's father,' he said curtly, resuming
his meal. 'He wants to meet you. He also wants to
talk to me about selling his land. I have invited him
over for dinner tomorrow.'

Lee said nothing. Already she felt sorry for the
older man, who had perhaps cherished dreams of his
daughter's marriage to Gilles. Dreams which must
surely have suffered a death blow now?

Their evenings had fallen into a regular pattern.
Lee knew she ought to be grateful for Gilles' absence,
but vague feelings of restlessness were beginning to
assail her. She had taken to spending a part of each
afternoon in the South Tower. From there she had an
excellent view of the fields, and had often, inadver-
tently, found her gaze straying to Gilles, tall, and
darkly handsome on the stallion he invariably rode,
the large hound at his heels, trained not to trespass
near the fragile vines.

It was June, and Lee did not need to be told how
critical this month was. Now unsettled weather could
mean uneven flowering of the vines, and a staggered
vintage; wind and rain could remove the pollen, im-
peding the pollination so vital to the production of the
grapes. It was no wonder that Gilles often stared
frowningly into the blue arc of the sky, his brow fur-
rowed in concentration as he listened to the weather
forecast before dinner, but Lee did not question him.
She was not going to be the one to put their marriage
on a more intimate footing. Gilles treated her as a

stranger, but in a household geared to the all-
important production of wine, this did not merit comment.

After a full stint in the fields by day, after dinner
Gilles went down to the wine cellars every evening
to check the wine levels in the vats, for with the onset
of the warmer weather there was a greater risk of
evaporation. Lee took no part in any of this. Gilles
had not even invited her to accompany him on an
inspection of the fields, even though he must know
of her interest. And she was not going to ask.

She had even grown accustomed to sharing a bed
with him, although she was always asleep when he
joined her in it, and he was gone long before she
opened her eyes in the morning.

CHAPTER FIVE

THERE was no real need to use the priceless Sèvres china for just the three of them, but Lee sensed that their guest would be flattered and proud to be treated with such distinction. The only time she had actually felt overwhelmed by the magnificence of the château was when Madame Le Bon had unlocked the china cupboards in a grim silence and allowed Lee to gaze at the treasures they concealed. Entire dinner services in Sèvres and Meissen china, designed specifically for the Chauvignys; vessels in solid gold and silver-gilt; not one but two ornate salts dating from the time when these were in constant use and also slightly more modern épergnes; cutlery such as Lee had never seen, with a delicate tracery of vines and grapes beaten on to them, the emblem of the house and seen everywhere, from the delicate scrolled gold design set into rich Imperial purple on one of the dinner services to the carving over the main entrance to the château; Chauvignys had drawn their wealth from the land since the dawn of time. There were cupboards packed with crystal as delicate and pure as clear water, and Lee had already instituted the beginnings of a system she had seen practised elsewhere; that of listing each precious heirloom, together with every occasion upon which it was used, although this last column in her book was as yet unmarked as the housekeeper had merely shrugged dismissively when Lee had asked for such details. The linen cupboards had also revealed a vast quantity of treasure, and Lee had personally supervised the washing and repairing of many of these items. It was with a feeling of intense pleasure that she wrote carefully in her book exactly what was being used tonight; although there would only be the three of them, this would be a practice run for the dinner party they were to give later in the week, and she was anxious for everything to go according to plan.

She was dressed and ready to receive their guest when Gilles entered their bedroom. He looked tired, lines of weariness drawn on either side of his mouth which Lee had not seen before.

'Is anything wrong?' The impulsive words were spoken before she could check them and she cringed mentally, awaiting the verbal mockery which was sure to follow.

To her surprise, Gilles didn't speak straight away. 'It's this weather,' he said at last. 'It's too hot, too soon; if we don't have rain soon we shall have to start manual watering; here at Chauvigny that won't be too much of a problem, but for the smaller growers like Jean-Paul... And if the weather doesn't break we run the risk of thunderstorms later in the year just before the vintage.'

Lee didn't need any explanation of those grim

words; she knew exactly, from her sojourn in Australia, what a heavy rain storm could do to the heavily ripened grapes.

There were no words of comfort she could offer which would not sound facile, and besides, she reminded herself, she was the last person Gilles would turn to to share his problems. The knowledge was like a knife in her breast, and before she had time to question why this should be so, Gilles was on his way to the bathroom, leaving her alone to grapple with the unfairness of the emotions which seemed to have taken root in her breast; emotions which, if she had any sense, she would smother instantly, she told herself, checking her appearance carefully in the mirror. She was wearing another of her new dresses, its elegant lines drawing attention to the slender shape of her body. She had caught her hair up in a chignon and as she examined it carefully for any loose hairs Gilles emerged from the bathroom, a towel draped nonchalantly around lean hips, the dark body hair curling and still damp. A sensation not unlike that experienced shooting upwards in a high-speed lift spiralled through Lee's stomach, followed by a lethargic weakness that had her clinging to the dressing table as Gilles frowned darkly.

'Oh come on,' he protested sardonically. 'This isn't the first time you've seen a near-nude male, and we both know it. Or is it because you've been deprived of any lovemaking for so long that you can't take your eyes off my body, Lee?'

She wanted to deny his accusations, but he had

moved within touching distance, his voice faintly husky as he probed demandingly, 'Would you like to touch me, Lee? To feel a man's body beneath your fingers again? Is that what you want? Is this?'

His hand caught her wrist and her fingers brushed the damp warmth of his chest, recoiling instantly, her eyes widening with the knowledge that she had found the momentary sensation deeply stirring. This was madness, she told herself weakly as she felt Gilles' breath on her neck. She was letting Gilles force her into the mould he had made for her, letting him trap her into reactions and emotions which were essentially foreign to her; and yet for one moment, with his warm male flesh beneath her fingers, she had almost forgotten why she was in this room; why Gilles had married her and what he thought of her.

'I must go. Our guest will be here soon.'

'So that's how you're going to play it, is it?' Gilles' savagery caught her off guard and she stared up at the angry face above her. 'A battle of wills, to see which of us can last out the longest? Well, it's a battle that you won't win, Lee,' he warned her as she opened the bedroom door, fleeing the insidious intimacy of their bedroom, and Gilles clad only in that brief towel which did so much to tantalise and so little to hide his very potent maleness.

Gilles had just joined her, dressed immaculately in a dinner suit and a crisp dress shirt, when their guest was announced, but to Lee's surprise he wasn't alone. Louise was with him. And as she went forward to greet them Lee shot a covert look at Gilles to see how he was reacting to this additional guest. Either he was an excellent actor, or he had lied to her about Louise, Lee thought, watching him bend to kiss the French-woman with every evidence of enjoyment.

She too was subjected to a similar embrace, the cold, hard blue eyes that Louise turned on her making her very much aware that she had not been forgiven for stealing the prize Louise had thought so securely hers.

Monsieur Trouville, Louise's father, on the other hand greeted Lee extremely courteously, his eyes so much like his daughter's but far kinder, appraising her thoroughly.

'You are a lucky man, Gilles, to have found such a bride,' he said at length, refusing an aperitif. 'Her eyes are the colour of a perfect Chardonnay grape.'

'You must be careful that they do not beguile you too easily, *mon ami*,' Louise interposed, darting Lee a malice-spiked glance. 'Your wife may have been known to you since childhood, but there have been years since then when you have been apart; when you have drunk deeply of the wine of life, and your wife has perhaps, without your knowledge, sipped at it too.'

'Louise! Please excuse my daughter. She is abusing the privilege of an old friendship. You would not wish Lee to think you envied her her husband, Louise,' Monsieur Trouville chided in a gentle voice, but with a note in it that made Lee wonder if he was as oblivious to Louise's personality as Gilles had suggested.

There had been unhappiness as well as anger in his eyes as they rested on Louise's hard face.

The dinner passed without incident. The meal was everything Lee had hoped it would be, and she had been meticulous about asking Gilles what wines he intended to serve so that the food would complement them.

Louise might have pushed away the crêpes Suzette and fresh strawberries served with whipped cream, but Gilles and Monsieur Trouville both evidently enjoyed the light sweet, and when after dinner Monsieur Trouville thanked her for the meal and suggested that he and Gilles retire to the latter's study for a business discussion Lee sensed that their guest wished to discuss Gilles' purchase of his land. This was confirmed when she and Louise were left alone and the latter commented spitefully.

'Gilles may feel that he has pulled the wool over Papa's eyes with this marriage, but I am not deceived.'

She prowled round the room while the men were gone, eyeing Lee's attractive flower arrangements disdainfully, and then when Madam Le Bon came in with the coffee Lee had requested, they exchanged a few words of conversation which, although Lee could not hear, she was sure related to her.

When the two men returned Gilles was looking far more relaxed than Lee had seen him looking for some time. He accepted a cup of coffee and their fingers touched accidentally, Lee withdrawing from the momentary contact as though she had been burned. Her reactions to Gilles were beginning to torment her even more than his disturbing presence. She looked up and found him studying her through narrowed eyes and her heart jolted.

'Gilles, you have not yet given Lee the earrings.' Louise's husky voice punctured the silence.

'Of course not.' Gilles glanced to the fireplace where the portrait of the Russian bride looked down at them. The girl had a sweetness of expression still alive today, and Lee noticed for the first time that in addition to the emerald ring she was wearing on her finger the girl was wearing matching earrings.

'Those come only with the first year of marriage, and the birth of the first child, surely you have not forgotten that, Louise?'

'Silly of me, I had. We must just hope that you are still around to wear them, mustn't we, Lee?' Louise commented sweetly.

'Louise!'

This time Monsieur Trouville really did sound angry, and Lee felt extremely sorry for him as he started to apologise for his daughter's bad behaviour.

'Don't worry about it, Bernard,' Gilles told him easily, placing his cup on the table and coming to slide the hard warmth of his arm round Lee's waist to draw her close to his side. 'Lee understands, don't you, *mignonne*?'

The endearment, the look of tender amusement in his eyes, caught her off guard, and her eyes widened and fastened on the gently smiling male lips, murmuring such blatant untruths. 'When people have as much as we do, they can afford to be generous, is that not so?' Gilles nuzzled the side of Lee's neck, apparently equally oblivious to Lee's start of surprise, and Louise's glittering fury. Only Monsieur Trouville appeared to regard the proceedings with any approval, his smile affectionate as he chided Gilles for embarrassing Lee in front of them.

'She is still too new a bride to accept embraces in public without thinking of those given in private,' their guest commented, further embarrassing Lee, 'and I sense by the look in your eyes, my friend, that we have already outstayed our welcome,' he added teasingly. 'I shall see my lawyer about the other business next week.'

Gilles went with them to their car, while Lee busied herself collecting the coffee cups and discarded glasses. When she heard Gilles' firm tread in the hall, her cheeks were still flushed, her pulses racing betrayingly.

'It's all right, you can drop the act; they've gone.' He was leaning against the doorway, his dress shirt a white blur in the darkness, his voice suddenly menacing as he taunted mockingly, 'Were you thinking of those embraces we had exchanged in private, my lovely bride? Perhaps I ought to reward you with some more if that is the effect they have on you. Bernard was most impressed. A beautiful, chaste child he called you.'

'I expect to Monsieur Trouville anyone under thirty is still a child,' Lee commented with more composure than she was feeling.

'He certainly is easy to fool.'

Lee ignored the taunting words.

'I'm glad you were able to settle your business sat-
isfactorily, Gilles, but I'm tired, and if you'll excuse
me, I'll go to bed.'

For once she wasn't asleep when he came into their
room, and she closed her eyes, forcing herself to
breathe evenly as he moved about the room, discarding clothes, showering, returning to slide beneath the
sheets, and even though she had her back to him and
her eyes were closed she knew instinctively that he
slept without any form of covering, and all the fears
and doubts she had had right from the start of their
'marriage' returned to haunt her. She was not indifferent to Gilles; how could she be? Her very first sexual stirrings had been aroused by him, and although
repressed and dammed all through her teenage years,
they were still there, ready to spring into new life at
his merest touch. At her side Gilles moved and a flood
of desire engulfed her. To her intense shame she knew
that if he turned to her now and took her in his arms
she would be powerless to prevent him from discovering exactly how wrong he was about her. But of
course, he was scarcely likely to do that!

The heatwave continued. Every day men were out
carefully watering and nurturing the vines. Gilles had
sent two of his own men to help Jean-Paul, and as
the earth grew dry and parched, waiting the reviving
caress of the life-giving rain, so did tension infiltrate
the atmosphere, until Lee felt as though her nerves
were stretched to breaking point.

The dinner they had given for Gilles' fellow *vignerons* had passed without comment. Most of the staff now seemed to accept her as the mistress of the château, and with Gilles' permission Lee had commissioned a firm of decorators to refurbish the ballroom. They had finished only that morning and Lee had been down to inspect the newly painted room. The colours were those in which the room had originally been painted—eau de nil and palest peach—and the room glowed softly in the afternoon sun. The floor had been stripped and re-waxed with a non-slip polish, for Lee was determined that the vintage dinner which would end her enforced stay at the château would be one which would be remembered long after she had been forgotten. There were to be forty guests for dinner, many of whom would be staying overnight. Gilles had already given her the invitation list and there were at least another hundred people who would be attending the ball afterwards. Gilles' position locally meant that the other winegrowers turned automatically to him for leadership.

When she left the ballroom, Lee went automatically to the South Tower. The beginnings of a headache made her feel muzzy and instead of going to her sitting room she climbed the extra stairs to the bedroom.

From here she could see for miles; the tiny bent figures of the men working on the vines; Gilles among them, working alongside his men to beat the drought which threatened to destroy the crop. The sunshine slanted oblongs of gold over the carpet, the hot early summer scents wafting in through the nar-

row window, and all at once Lee wanted to be outside.

Discarding her elegant linen dress in favour of
jeans and thin tee-shirt, she hurried through the courtyard and through the vines, aromatic from their recent
watering.

Beyond the formal gardens of the château and the
fields of vines stretched a small wooden copse where
Gilles rode most mornings, and without being aware
of it, Lee followed the dusty, dry path until she was
swallowed up by the cool green interior of the
shadow-dappled sanctuary from the sun's molten
glare.

The stream which fed the château's elaborate water
gardens had dried to a small trickle, but it was still
pleasant to lie and listen to the clean sound of the
water. Drowsy and more at peace than she had been
since coming to the château, Lee closed her eyes.

When she opened them again her first thought was
that she must have slept for hours, it was so dark, and
then she realised that the darkness was the heavy,
sullen clouds which had covered the sky. She got up,
brushing twigs and grass from her jeans, shivering
under the cooling breeze which had suddenly sprung
up. A glance at her watch told her that she was already late for dinner, and as she searched for the path
which had led her into the copse the first peal of thunder sounded overhead, followed by lightning which
rent the sky in two.

Her first thought was relief that now they would
have rain, followed by the wry knowledge that she

would be soaked by the time she returned to the château. Thunderstorms had never frightened Lee; on the contrary she found them exhilarating as though all the electricity generated by the celestial activity was mirrored in some small way by her own body.

For a moment she stood with her face uplifted, welcoming the touch of the rain as it pattered down on to the leaves, and then she turned, transfixed by the sight of the motionless horse and rider guarding the exit from the small clearing where she had been sleeping.

'Gilles!' She moved towards him, noticing the way his shirt clung damply to his shoulders, his dark hair sprinkled with moisture and curling slightly.

Another clap of thunder obliterated her voice, and the stallion reared angrily, pawing the air with rolling eyes.

'Where the hell have you been, damn you?' Gilles swore, dismounting angrily. Lee's eyes were riveted on the tanned breadth of the shoulders beneath the damp shirt. The trees had obviously protected her from the worst of the rain.

'I fell asleep...'

How inane it sounded, with the thunder rolling overhead and lightning stabbing the sky, and a rueful smile curved her lips.

'Don't laugh at me!' he ground out furiously. 'I've been searching for you for two hours. One of the men saw you leaving the château...'

'Where did you think I'd gone?'

His anger puzzled her, but his reply was drowned

out by another clap of thunder, more vicious this time. The stallion reared angrily, screaming shrill defiance at the elements, and then with flashing hooves was gone, leaving them alone in the clearing.

'Your horse…'

'He'll be all right. He'll make straight for his stable. Satan doesn't like the rain, which is more than I can say for you. Doesn't the thunder frighten you?'

Lee laughed, 'No, I love it, it's so exhilarating. Does it frighten you?'

There was no reply. Gilles was studying her closely.

'I suppose I should have guessed that,' he muttered hoarsely. 'Anything as elemental and passion-filled as this would excite you, wouldn't it? Very well, Lee, I give in…'

He reached for her as he spoke, his mouth covering hers and destroying all her determinedly erected barriers; the storm and Gilles seemed to meld and become one entity before which she was helpless, and as Gilles' mouth forced hers to part in soft surrender she thought fleetingly of the mother of the Greek hero Theseus who had claimed that her son had been conceived by Poseidon, the sea-god, who had come to her in a dream; such elemental desire as she was feeling now was surely God-given, and as Gilles lowered her on to the still dry grass of the small glade she made no attempt to hinder him. Droplets of rain from his hair had fallen to his shoulders and throat and she raised herself up lightly to savour them with her tongue, tasting the cool dampness with eyes that wondered at the sudden darkening of the iron-grey ones above her.

It was as though she were lost in a dream, driven by some elemental force above and beyond the sensible motives which had hitherto ruled her life. She felt no shame as Gilles tugged impatiently at her tee-shirt and jeans, even revelling in the look in his eyes when he at last gazed at her naked body. His head bent towards her and she knew he intended to kiss her, but instead she placed her finger to his lips and slowly began unfastening the buttons of his shirt, following the progress of her fingers, with light butterfly kisses which drew a hoarse moan from between his gritted teeth and invoked a punishment which left her clinging mindlessly to his broad shoulders while his lips and hands left her in no doubt of his urgent need to possess her.

Above them the thunder rolled and crashed, lightning splitting the night sky, but Lee was oblivious; some pagan part of herself she had never dreamed existed was driving her on towards the culmination of all those emotions she had experienced since coming to the château but never fully understood. Now, with her fingers delicately exploring the hard warmth of Gilles' flesh, she did, and for a moment she was still as she tasted the knowledge which after the initial sweetness was as bitter as Eve's apple. She loved Gilles! Something deep down inside her shuddered and rose up in a tidal wave and she knew beyond any shadow of a doubt that this moment, this passionate, almost violent culmination of a love which had begun over six years ago, was something that nothing could stop. A vivid flash of lightning touched their bodies, Gilles' so male, the skin darkly tanned, her own, softly curved, pliant, female; all around them, infusing the very air they breathed, was the smell of the grapes, of earth coming to life beneath the rain; the moisture touched their skins, but Lee barely noticed. She moaned softly in pleasure, her frantic movements against Gilles' body destroying the last remnants of his self-control, so that he cursed harshly against her mouth and then possessed it endlessly, breaking the kiss only when his breathing had grown harsh and ragged.

Tonight she was not Lee Raven, nor even Gilles' wife, Lee told herself hazily; she was woman, a creature who had enticed and aroused man until he was driven by the need to capture her elusiveness in the only way he could—by possessing her, and with the thunder charging the air around them she arched instinctively beneath Gilles, knowing with a knowledge that went deeper than mere experience that this time there would be no holding back.

Later she would be astounded at the intensity of her passion, at the memory of how she had wantonly caressed every inch of Gilles' taut body, mutely inciting him to repeat his earlier demanding arousal of her flesh with the hard warmth of his lips and hands. At one point he had wound his hand in her hair, pulling away from her to study the swelling curves of her breasts, the creamy skin of her stomach and the tender line of her thighs, before parting them deliberately

with his own in a way that made her heart jerk on its
first shaft of fear, soon lost beneath the heated possession of his kiss as he murmured that her skin possessed the bloom of grapes, and her mouth tasted as
potent as the richest wine in his cellars.

He possessed her with an urgency that brought
pain, shadowing her eyes as they flew open, his own
shocked, and then glazing as the thunder rolled overhead, and he and the storm became one, carrying her
far beyond pain to a place where nothing existed but
the fierce waves of pleasure created by Gilles' touch;
a pleasure which spiralled and exploded, leaving her
feeling as though she was floating somewhere on a
soft, warm cloud.

She could hear Gilles breathing close beside her,
the sound tortured as he dragged air into his lungs.
Her body was damp from the rain and the grass and
all at once she felt cold.

'You were a virgin!' The words were coldly ac-
cusing and she turned her head away. 'My God, you
little bitch! If it was experience you wanted... Here,
put these on.'

She dressed without looking at him, her earlier ex-
hilaration swamped by the sickness which had invaded her. What had she expected? That he would
take her in his arms and swear undying love? That he
would say his possession of her was the most beautiful thing he had ever experienced? No doubt the
caresses which had sent her into such a frenzy of
delight were commonplace to him. Her clothes were
damp and her fingers trembled over them. She longed

to look at Gilles and yet daren't in case he read the
truth in her eyes. Now, with passion spent, her body
was beginning to ache, and as she pulled the tee-shirt
over her head she saw the beginnings of bruises on
her breast. Gilles had seen them too, and he grasped
her wrist and grimaced in disgust. 'Like the grapes,
you bruise easily, Madam la Comtesse. What the hell
were you playing at?' he burst out impatiently as
though no longer able to conceal his anger. He had
his jeans on, his shirt held in one hand so that Lee's
eyes were fixed on the tanned column of his throat,
and the pulse beating there; a pulse she had not so
long ago touched with her lips and felt burst into urgent life beneath them. She dragged her eyes away.

'Why didn't you tell me?'

'Would you have believed me? You needn't worry
that this means I want to hold you to our marriage,
Gilles.' He was watching her sardonically. Had he
thought she had suddenly decided to force his hand
in the hope that once he discovered she was a virgin
he would continue the marriage? Did he think she had
been swayed by the knowledge of his material possessions, or worse still, had he guessed that she had
fallen in love with him?

'You condemned me years ago on a letter that
wasn't even written by me,' she told him slowly.
'What happened tonight, happened, and I feel no
shame that it did.' She raised her head proudly, willing her eyes not to give her away, not to betray to
the waiting man exactly how she felt about him.
'What we did brought me great pleasure, Gilles,' she

said bravely, 'and I see no reason why I should feel ashamed of that.'

She heard his harsh, indrawn breath, and the black fury leaping into his eyes, as he turned on his heel and said curtly, 'Well, next time you feel like experimenting with something as dangerous as sex, find yourself another partner—I don't like feeling that I'm some sort of stud animal!'

He was gone, leaving her to find her own way back to the château, her dreams lying broken at her feet, as he left her in no doubt as to how he regarded what had, for her, been the most poetically beautiful moments of her life. There had been something about their union which had struck a chord so deep and primitive that she doubted that it would ever be struck again.

Unhappily she made her way back to the château. No one questioned her absence or damp clothes and hair, but there was no sign of Gilles. Refusing any supper, she went up to their room, and although she lay awake well into the small hours he never came in. That night for the first time she slept alone.

CHAPTER SIX

LEE had just finished writing to Drew, telling him that their engagement was off. She could not return his ring as yet because Gilles still had it. In her letter she had explained that she had fallen in love with someone else. No need for him to know of her marriage to Gilles; that was not something which could be told in a letter.

Soon it would be time for the vintage; already the grapes were ripening in the hot August sun, while a harvest of another kind grew slowly inside her.

She had known within a week that she was pregnant, and after the first initial shock had come a sweet piercing pleasure that she was carrying Gilles' child; a child conceived on that one night of elemental fusing. She touched her stomach gently. As yet only the most discerning person could tell that she carried a child. It was there in the faint rounding of her stomach and the fullness of her breasts; the slightly altered shape of her face, but that was all. She had been sick several times in the morning, but because Gilles slept in the dressing room and left the château long before she was awake in the morning he did not know. And that was the way she wanted it to stay. For the child's sake Gilles might insist that they continue the marriage, and her heart, starving for his tenderness, overburdened with her love for him, could not endure that. Another month and she would be gone, and her secret with her. She had become very dreamy, spending her afternoons lazily in the South Tower, dreaming of her child's birth.

Soon the grape pickers would be with them, students in the main, and casual labour, and Lee had already gone over the dormitories above the stables and garages to check that everything was in order for their arrival.

Jean-Paul drove into the courtyard in a battered Citroën one sultry afternoon when Lee was catnapping in her room. Although the baby had as yet made scant difference to her figure, already she was beginning to feel tired.

'It's the baby!' he yelled excitedly when Lee went downstairs, awoken by the noisy disturbance of his arrival. 'I've taken Marie-Thérèse to the hospital and I came here to ask Gilles if he could lend me Henri until the baby arrives. Our grapes are ready for picking, but if I am not there to supervise...' He shrugged, meaning that with the cheap labour which was all he could afford the grapes could be spoiled by ignorant careless hands if he was not there on hand.

'I'm sure he will,' Lee said impulsively. 'He's in the cellar, I think, inspecting last year's wine. They think it's ready to be bottled. I'll come with you, Jean-Paul,' she added on impulse. After all, wasn't she knowledgeable enough about wines to merit an inspection of Gilles' treasured cellars?

The cellars stretched endlessly beneath the château; huge stainless steel vats standing ready to receive this year's harvest; casks containing the previous year's wine lining the long, dark cavern where the temperature was thermostatically controlled to provide exactly the right temperature for the maturing wine. Lee shivered when they walked from the bright, hot sunshine outside into the shadowed cavernous entrance to the cellars which seemed to yawn widely like some giant maw.

'You're cold!' Jean-Paul exclaimed. 'I can find my own way, Lee.'

'No, it's all right, I want to come with you.'

Jean-Paul looked at her and smiled hugely. 'Ah, I understand.'

'What do you understand, *mon ami*?' Gilles drawled from behind them.

Lee gave a sudden start—she hadn't seen him approach, her eyes still unaccustomed to the dark of the cellars.

'I understand that your beautiful young wife is anxious not to miss the opportunity to snatch a few extra minutes of her husband's time.'

Lee's cheeks burned, and she was glad of the darkness to conceal her betraying flush. Was she so obvious? She could not deny that hidden at the back of her mind had been a desire to see Gilles, even if she ultimately was forced to endure his total disinterest in her presence.

'Aren't you going to kiss her?' Jean-Paul teased. 'Many times when we were first married, Marie-Thérèse would bring my lunch out to the fields, and for a while we would forget about the vines.' He smiled reminiscently, while Gilles arched his eyebrows and said sardonically to Lee,

'Is that why you came down here? So that I could kiss you?'

Lee laughed lightly,

'No, of course not. Jean-Paul wanted to ask for your help, Gilles. Marie-Thérèse has started with the baby...'

She left the two men to talk while she examined the cellar more thoroughly. It was really time that she lost this irrational, childish fear of enclosed dark spaces, she thought firmly, when she had turned for the third time to check that the door was still open behind her.

'...so Henry will go back with you and set the men to work.' Gilles was saying when she got back. 'And, *mon ami*!' he clapped Jean-Paul on the back, 'this year the vintage will be a good one, fit to put down for twenty-one years, for your son's coming of age, *non*?'

'Marie-Thérèse might have a girl,' Lee protested, incensed by this evidence of male chauvinism, although she herself dreamed constantly of a child with his father's dark hair and eyes.

'And next year we shall celebrate the birth of your child, *non*?' Jean-Paul teased Gilles, and for a second Lee paled, terrified that he might have guessed her

secret. She need not have worried, Jean-Paul was totally concerned with his wife and his vineyard in that
order, and within an hour of his arrival he was on his
way with Gilles' most experienced foreman.

'You will need Henri soon yourself,' Lee commented. 'Your own grapes...'

'Please allow me to know the condition of my
grapes,' Gilles bit out curtly, turning on his heel and
leaving her alone in the courtyard. Several minutes
later she heard the impatient sound of the stallion's
hooves over the cobbles and glancing upwards had a
momentary impression of taut, angry strength as
Gilles rode past her, his face an iron mask in which
only his eyes seemed to be alive, hating her with a
ferocity that was like a knife in her heart.

He did not return for dinner, and Lee, knowing that
tremendous strength and fiery temper of the stallion,
grew worried. She could barely touch her own food,
and when the phone rang she leapt up, convinced that
Gilles must have had an accident.

It was Louise on the other end of the line, and Lee
barely listened to what the other woman was saying
until she heard Gilles' name, and then her fingers
gripped the receiver until they were white as she listened to Louise telling her that Gilles was having dinner with them and would not be returning until late.

There was triumph in the other woman's voice, and
Lee wondered if Gilles had changed his mind about
Louise as she replaced the receiver, or did he simply
think it was safe to indulge his physical needs with

her now that she could not pressure him into marriage?

Alone in the huge bed she tossed and turned. She could not continue as she was much longer. Already the strain of her love for Gilles was etching dark shadows beneath her eyes, and although her skin was tanned by the sun, she was losing weight. Her hands went instinctively to the soft fullness of her stomach and the new life cradled safely there. It was nearly three months since the night when the child had been conceived. She had visited a doctor in Nantes, supposedly to have her hair trimmed, and what she had learned from him had reassured her as to her health and that of the child she carried. She had followed his advice minutely and religiously taken the vitamins he had given her.

That weekend the pickers arrived, and life at the château centred around the vines. Heavy storms had been predicted and it would be a race against time to get the grapes in before they broke.

Lee worked hard in the kitchen supervising the preparation of meals for the pickers, often going out into the fields to help with the picking when she had a spare moment. The work was hard and hot under the merciless sun which seemed to beat down from an intensely blue sky, and like the other girls Lee took the precaution of covering her head while she worked.

Her experience in Australia had taught her the importance of swift, knowledgeable picking, and when Gilles rode along the vines on which she was working one hot afternoon, she didn't stop working to talk to him, her fingers flying deftly from vine to basket, with the rhythmic ease of the experienced picker.

'What the hell do you think you're doing?' He had dismounted from the stallion and seized her under the armpits, dragging her away from the other workers, his face livid with rage.

'Picking grapes. What did you think?' Lee asked flippantly. He looked so angry that for a moment she thought he was going to hit her.

'My wife does not pick grapes!'

For a moment she was stunned.

'Oh, don't be so ridiculous, Gilles,' she said coolly when she had her breath back. 'Storms are forecast, and with Henri and two other men helping Jean-Paul, you need every hand you can get in the fields, and mine at least are experienced.'

She glanced at their smooth palms as she spoke, her fingers stained and her nails dirty. Gilles followed the small movement, his fingers curling round her slender wrists as he too surveyed the sunburnt flesh.

'You are determined to turn me into a monster, aren't you?' he demanded savagely. He was white under his tan, his eyes no longer grey, but the purple blackness of the Syrah grape, which according to legend had been brought to the Rhone valley from Shiraz by a returning Crusader. 'Do you want my people to say that I work you until you are ill? Have you looked at yourself recently?'

A deep flush of humiliation settled on Lee's cheeks. She knew she looked less than glamorous in her ancient jeans and checked shirt, but she had honestly wanted to help Gilles, to play her part in the gathering of the harvest so that no matter what the future might bring, the wine they made this vintage would owe something, no matter how meagre, to her.

'Oh, for God's sake!' Gilles groaned suddenly, dragging her into his arms and kissing her until she was gasping for breath. As savagely as she had been taken prisoner she was released, to stand blinking in the sun while all around them the pickers laughed and joked. She touched her swelling mouth with trembling fingers as Gilles remounted. Of course, he had had to kiss her to prevent the pickers from thinking they were quarrelling. Gossip spread like wildfire when the pickers were in evidence, and Gilles would not want Louise to suspect that their marriage was cracking up. He had made no comment about the evening he had stayed at their house, and looking into his thunderous face Lee could only think that if he had gone to Louise to relieve his frustration the remedy could not have been very effective.

She was still standing staring up at him when he leaned down and swung her up before him.

'I'm taking you back to the château,' he said abruptly. 'And then you're going to rest. The picking will be finished tomorrow and then we start the pressing. The pickers have to move on to another vineyard when they finish here, so there won't be time for the usual celebrations this year—not with the weather threatening to break, but we still have the buyers to entertain, and I don't want you making yourself ill picking grapes.'

Because he needed a hostess, Lee reminded herself. How could she ever have been stupid enough to think he was taking her home because he was concerned about her? But for a brief, ecstatic moment that was exactly what she had thought!

'Relax,' she was instructed as the huge stallion obeyed his master's command to walk. 'Satan isn't used to carrying females. Lean back against me, that will lessen the discomfort.'

Before the animal had taken more than a few paces Lee had begun to feel distinctly queasy, and was too grateful for Gilles' suggestion to question it. It was only when one arm came round her to hold her securely against his chest and the other grasped the reins loosely that she realised just how intimately she was pressed against him. It was impossible to avoid touching him, however, and her nostrils were filled with the warm male scent of him as they rode into the courtyard and he swung her down to the floor.

'There's no need to come inside with me,' she protested when he walked with her into the shadowed hall.'

'Allow me to decide what it necessary for myself, Lee.' His eyes raked her pale slenderness. 'You look as though you're starving yourself to death. Are you ill?'

'Of course not!' If one didn't count unrequited love as an illness, for that was what was responsible for her wan cheeks and lack of appetite. Even sleep was sometimes an impossibility, lying alone in a bed meant for loving while Gilles slept in the dressing room.

'Louise and her father will be attending the buyers' dinner, and in view of the number of guests we shall have staying with us, I think it might be advisable if we returned to our previous sleeping arrangements.'

The curt words caught Lee off guard. She stiffened, hope trembling through her. 'You mean…'

'I mean that we shall sleep together, Lee, simply that and nothing more.' He said it curtly, so curtly that Lee suspected that he was warning her not to try and divert him from his chosen path. She coloured again. What did he think she was? So depraved that she would deliberately seek his rejection?

Lee had spent many hours over the menu for the banquet to be served to the buyers. As the main purpose of the banquet was to provide a suitable accompaniment for Gilles' wines, Lee consulted with him over her final menu.

For the first course, she intended to serve merlans frits en lorgnette, a delicious fish dish which would complement their local wines, followed by casserole de cailles aux morilles, a delicacy of which Lee knew the French were inordinately fond, quail cooked with tiny mushroom-like morels; for the sweet course there would be soufflé Grand Marnier, followed by regional cheese for those with a less sweet tooth. Gilles frowned a little over the final menu, suggesting that she might be trying to take on too much. Lee didn't tell him about the sister-in-law who ran her own restaurant and who had passed much of her knowledge on to Lee when she had stayed with them in Australia. She had already discussed her plans with the cook, who visualised no problems, and as the plans Lee had been carefully laying for the last few months were meticulously followed, she felt she had every right to feel proud of her achievements.

Beds were made up with the linen which had been washed and aired weeks before, bedrooms, already cleaned and prepared, were stripped of the coverings protecting highly polished and valuable furniture. The florists Lee had visited in Nantes arrived and potted plants and shrubs were cleverly arranged in the ballroom. Musicians had been hired and carefully briefed, and when the clothes she had ordered from Orléans arrived, she examined them in satisfaction. The idea was not new; costume balls were always a firm favourite with women and had been for centuries, but this was one with a difference, because she and Gilles would be playing parts which had been played before—by a young Russian girl and her handsome, dashing husband. Whatever hopes had been in her heart when she planned this ball, as meticulously true in every detail to that held so long ago to celebrate the marriage of that other couple, Lee now acknowledged that these were dead, but at least she could have the satisfaction of knowing that this vantage would last for ever in the memories of those who attended it.

No one was forgotten, and even the chattering girls in the kitchen had their attractive striped dresses and starched, frilly aprons.

'Oh, madame, it is all so exciting!' one exclaimed as she assisted Lee with the flowers she was arranging for the guest bedrooms.

Gilles had raised his eyebrows slightly at first when Lee told him of her plans, but he had consented easily enough; he probably had too much on his mind to concern himself with such minor matters, Lee conceded. Her one disappointment was that Marie-Thérèse and Jean-Paul would not be coming. Their new, precious daughter could not be left, and although regretful they had been adamant about remaining at home. As she too would have been in their place, Lee thought, her hands going instinctively to her stomach. It had become a reflex action these days, and Gilles who had walked into the bedroom while she was on her knees examining the costumes frowned slightly.

'Is something wrong?'

What would he say if she told him, 'Nothing, your son has just kicked me?' Lee wondered half-hysterically; instead she shook her head, refusing to give in to the clamouring longing to look at the man standing over her, to feast her eyes on his virile maleness.

'Then will you stop acting like the victim of a rape?' he demanded acidly. 'Because God knows, Lee, you were willing enough…you…'

'Please don't talk about it, Gilles,' she protested quickly. 'I'm sorry if I've ever given you the impression that…'

'That you wanted me?' he cursed savagely. 'Well, you damned well did, Lee…you damned well did!'

He had gone before she could finish what she had been going to say, which was simply that she had never wanted to give him the impression that she considered herself a victim of any type, unless it was of her ever-growing love for him. Their lovemaking, which for her had been so pleasurable and was so cherished, to him appeared to be something which he bitterly resented—hated almost, and slow tears slid down her face as she acknowledged that her love was completely and utterly hopeless.

Everything was in readiness for the arrival of their guests. Lee found her feet leading her towards the tower room which had become her own personal sanctuary. Gilles was in the cellars checking on the fermentation of the new wine, and she had several hours to herself before the first of their guests would arrive.

She was too drowsy to concentrate and the thought of the cool green bed in the room above was tempting. In the upper room she removed the cool linen dress she had been wearing. Her reflection glimpsed in the mirror showed that she would not be able to keep her secret much longer—and indeed could not have kept it this long had she and Gilles truly been man and wife. She lay down on the bed, pulling the silk coverlet over herself with a small sigh. Soon she would be gone from the château. 'Until the vintage,' Gilles had said, and with this dinner party and ball it would be over. Her eyes ached with unshed tears, her hands going protectively to her stomach. For a few moments she allowed herself to fantasise about how

different things would have been were they really
married. How cherished and protected she would have
been then. Gilles would want to take no chances; the
baby she carried might well be the heir to the Chauvigny estates. But how would he have viewed her
actual pregnancy? Would he have been pleased by the
evidence of his virility, but slightly remote? Yes, she
was sure this would have been his reaction. She
sighed again, letting sleep enfold her. Madame Le
Bon had been particularly difficult lately, and Lee was
terrified that the other woman would discover her
condition, without really knowing why she should be;
she only knew that with the discovery her annoyance
at Madame Le Bon's animosity had given way to a
creeping fear.

'Lee!'

Someone was calling her name, dragging her back
from the dreams which were so much more pleasant
than reality. She opened her eyes and looked straight
into the angry grey ones of her husband.

'What are you doing here? Our guests will be arriving shortly!'

He was still dressed in his working clothes, the
smell of fermenting grapes clinging richly to his skin,
his jaw shadowed with the faint beginnings of his
beard. Lee's throat felt dry, and she swallowed nervously, shaken by a longing to reach up and touch
the stubbled skin.

'Lee?' There was enquiry as well as impatience in
the word.

'Yes, I'm awake. I'll get dressed and then go and get changed.'

'Dressed?'

She had meant the words only as a warning that she wanted him to leave, but they seemed to spark off a minor explosion. Gilles' eyes darkened as, far from leaving the room, he came farther into it, and Lee was glad that she had taken the precaution of closing the curtain as he reached for her with hard hands, pinning her on to the mattress as he demanded harshly.

'You mean to tell me you are undressed? With the door unlocked and anyone free to walk in?'

His anger bewildered her.

'No one would just walk in,' she protested. 'All the staff know that I like to be alone during the afternoons.'

'Why? So that you can dream of your fiancé? What would he say if he knew that you have given yourself to me? Or don't you mean to tell him until it's too late?'

'That's a vile thing to suggest!'

'Then you have told him? Well, perhaps I ought to give you something else to tell him,' he said softly before Lee could tell him that she had broken her engagement. His hands had already slid up from her arms, one grasping the thin silk cover while the other stroked her throat.

She opened her mouth to protest, but the scent of him filled her nostrils, and instead of repudiating him, her lips parted trustingly for his kiss. She loved him so much that she ached for his touch; longed for him to possess her with tenderness and love.

There was anger in his kiss and she tried to pull away, realisation of what he actually felt coming too late. His hands held her face, and she had to close her eyes against the anger she saw smouldering there.

'Look at me!' The harsh command jerked them open again. 'It is I who is making love to you,' Gilles told her, 'so don't close your eyes and pretend it is someone else.' She heard him swear suddenly, and then the protective cover was wrenched away completely, his mouth moist and urgent against her drowsy skin, waves of pleasure sweeping over her and obliterating her willpower.

There was something almost driven in the way Gilles kissed her and touched her; as though his actions were dictated by something stronger than the commands of his brain. Perhaps his own self-enforced celibacy was proving too much for him, she thought hazily as his hands cupped her breasts, fuller now and tender. His harsh groan was smothered against her flesh, his lips hot and dry against the coolness of her skin. An overwhelming tide of love swamped her as she looked down at the darkness of his head against her breast. His body felt damp, and drops of perspiration stood out of his forehead as he dragged himself away, his eyes almost black as he studied the shadowy outline of her breasts, the nipples hard and aroused.

He muttered something in French which she could not catch, and Lee knew that he was despising himself

for wanting her body, when he felt nothing but contempt for her as a person. She moved away from him,
bitterly hurt by the realisation that his desire for her
sprang from man's basest instinct, but with a harsh
cry he seized her in his arms, holding her against the
length of a body that shook with pent-up need, his
face dark and congested.

His kiss blanketed out everything but her answering desire. Her lips parted tremulously as he probed
and demanded access to the sweet moistness they
were concealing. With heated urgency his hands
stroked her body, and Lee, almost mindless with the
pleasure they were inducing, forgot that such intimacy
might betray her condition. The touch of his tongue
against her nipples provoked a small gasped cry, answered in the heated pressure of his body. Her nails
raked the smooth flesh of his back, her lips moaning
soft pleas for fulfilment, which found an answer in
the heated shudder of Gilles' body above her. Their
situation, Gilles' lack of love for her, all faded into
insignificance, and it was only the sudden slamming
of a car door in the courtyard that jerked Lee back
into awareness. She froze in Gilles' arms.

'Gilles!'

'What is it? If you're remembering your untrusting
fiancé it's too damned late,' his desire-drugged voice
informed her.

'I think your guests are arriving. I just heard a car
door.'

Her shaky words had the desired effect.

'What?'

Lee felt the cool air shaft over her body as he left the bed. He glanced out of the window, and then without looking at her strode to the door, pulling on his shirt as he did so.

'I'll go and talk to them while you get changed. Don't take too long.'

Not a word about what had occurred between them, but what had she been expecting?

It took her longer than usual to shower and dress. Her fingers felt unusually clumsy, and her brain was still clouded by the unappeased desire Gilles had aroused within her. She was wearing one of her new couture gowns, glad of its elegant, flowing lines, skimming the soft curves of her body and drawing attention to her lissom shape.

She went downstairs nervously. Gilles smiled at her as she entered the salon—a smile which illuminated his harsh features, almost taking her breath away. For a moment she was actually in danger of forgetting that this was only a charade for the benefit of his guests, and her whole body trembled as he drew her within the curve of his arm, proudly presenting her to his friends.

More guests were arriving. The women were elegant as only Parisienne women can be, the men, urbane and charming, speaking in delightfully accented English as they complimented Gilles on his choice of bride.

While the men discussed wine, Lee offered to show their wives to their rooms. She could tell that beneath the polite façade the women were curious about her, and she answered their discreet questions as ably as she could, using Gilles' story that their relationship had been founded when she was in her teens. A little to her amusement they seemed to approve of such an arrangement.

When she returned to the drawing room their guests of honour had arrived—the Junior Minister for Trade, and his wife.

'A masked ball is such a delightful idea,' Madam Lefleur commented with a smile when she and Lee were introduced. 'I congratulate you on your originality.'

Lee was immediately drawn to the soignée Frenchwoman, and as they preceded Gilles and her husband up the graceful sweep of stairs, she explained how she had got the idea from the portrait of Gilles' ancestor.

'A very dashing-looking rogue,' Madame Lefleur laughed, pausing so that Lee could open the door to the suite of rooms she had had prepared for these honoured guests. Busily talking to her companion, it was several seconds before Lee saw the chaos to which the room had been reduced, and by that time it was too late to close the door up, because Madame Lefleur too had seen the disruption of the elegant sitting room—dead flowers heaped untidily on the table, the hearth covered in ashes, furniture all awry, and easily glimpsed through the connecting door, the unmade bed in the next room carelessly heaped with bolsters and sheets. Lee started to tremble. What on earth had happened? She had been at such pains to make sure all the rooms were immaculate, and these important guests had been given the most luxurious suite. She closed her eyes, half believing that she was seeing things, then opened them again, as she heard Gilles' deep tones behind her. He would be furious with her!

To Lee's everlasting gratitude, before she could say or do anything Madame Lefleur stepped smoothly in front of her and smiled charmingly at Gilles.

'Isn't that stupid of me, I think I must have left my handbag downstairs. Would you be an angel, Gilles, and get it for me. Lazy of me, I know, but that staircase of yours is so very long! You go with him, Georges,' she instructed her husband. 'You know where I was sitting.'

When they had gone she smiled impishly at Lee. 'I left my bag in the auto, but by the time I have remembered that you will have time to explain to me what is happening.'

'I don't know,' Lee admitted slowly. A suspicion was beginning to take root in her mind, but surely Madame Le Bon would not be foolish enough to put her own security at risk in such a way?

'I think perhaps I do,' Madame Lefleur said comprehendingly. 'Ours is a rather small circle and one gets to know people very well. I detect Louise's hand behind this affair. Am I not right? She has made it very plain in the past that she considers Gilles to be her own personal property. It was no secret that she expected to marry him. And I seem to remember her once telling me that Gilles' housekeeper had once worked for her. This sort of trick is typical of Louise.'

'I'll get one of the maids up here to tidy up this mess,' Lee began, smothering a small gasp as the door was suddenly thrust open and Gilles stood there, his eyes darkening as they slowly surveyed the carnage.

'Gilles, your wife has been the victim of a most unpleasant piece of mischief,' Madame Lefleur said quickly before Gilles could speak. 'The poor girl is white with the shock of it.' Her eyes suddenly widened with remorse as she looked at Lee. '*Ma chère*, forgive me if I have spoken out of turn. Perhaps you did not know about Louise…'

'Lee knows all about her,' Gilles cut in abruptly. 'But you cannot seriously be suggesting that she walked in here and did this!'

'Not her, but a certain someone who has her interests at heart,' Madame Lefleur told him wisely. 'Did you find my handbag?'

'No. Georges remembered that you left it in the car. He has gone to get it.'

'Then we shall all go downstairs and drink some more of your excellent sherry,' Madame Lefleur said placidly, 'and while we are doing so your maids can undo this mischievous meddling.' She turned to leave the room and Lee made to follow her, but the shock of discovering the housekeeper's malicious destruction, coupled with the earlier events of the afternoon, plus the rush to get ready, all combined to make her feel exceedingly dizzy. She clutched the door for support, her face so white that Madame Lefleur hurried anxiously to her side.

'*Petite*, it is not the end of the world. Tell her this is so, Gilles,' she insisted, 'instead of standing there glowering like a tyrant! The poor child is close to fainting. Gilles, where is your room?'

Once in motion, Madame was as impossible to stop as an avalanche. Lee was swept back to her room. A *tisane* was ordered, and Gilles was banished to take care of his guests, while Lee recovered.

'It is a difficult time when one carries one's first *bébé*,' Madame Lefleur commented reminiscently.

Lee's cup clattered on to her saucer, her eyes round and frightened. She had thought her secret so safe, but the knowing eyes of another woman had perceived the truth instantly.

'No wonder Gilles frowned so,' Madame continued blithely. 'You must take care, *petite*.'

'Gilles doesn't know!' Now what on earth had made her say that? Lee bowed her head, unable to hold back her tears any longer. Wisely Madame Lefleur let her cry.

'All is not well between you,' she said at last, 'but there is love, Lee, I can tell that, and where there is love, there must also be life, *non*?' she enquired gently, touching Lee's stomach lightly, 'and hope. Now, you will dry your eyes, put on your make-up and go downstairs with your head held high, and your housekeeper will be left to wonder why her little plan has provoked no response. *Non*?'

'Where there is love...' The words kept repeating

themselves as Lee prepared for the ball. But her love alone was not enough; and besides, Gilles did not want her. She was just a screen he was hiding behind to protect himself from Louise—Louise, his spurned mistress who had quite deliberately tried to make Lee look foolish in front of Gilles' important guests. How would *she* react when she discovered that her plans had gone awry?

Lee sighed, trying to push all personal thoughts to the back of her mind so that she could concentrate on the evening ahead.

Those guests who were staying overnight were now in their rooms preparing for dinner and the ball which would follow. Lee had already been down to check the dinner table and the ballroom, anxious lest Madame Le Bon had planned any other unpleasant surprises, but everything had been in order. She could hear Gilles moving about in the dressing room. Her dress lay across the bed, a mist of sea-green chiffon, cut low across the breasts in the Regency style, with tiny puff sleeves embroidered with pearls. Pearls for tears, she thought bleakly. She had caught her hair up on top of her head in soft ringlets, pale green ribbons threaded through them, and as Gilles emerged from the dressing room, she saw him studying her reflection in the mirror, his lips curving sardonically as he glanced from her to the gown lying on the bed.

'It is almost fitting that we should take the parts of René and his Russian bride,' he murmured cynically, 'Our circumstances are very similar. He too forced his bride into marriage.'

'But he eventually loved her.' There was more pain than Lee knew in the low words. Gilles studied her downbent head for several seconds before replying coolly, 'And she loved him—or so the romantics would have us believe.'

'But you of course know better?'

His eyebrows rose, his eyes lingering on her flushed cheeks and small fists. 'Surely you aren't saying that she *could* love him? A man who ravished her away from her family and home? A man…like me.' His voice was harsh and Lee felt her breathing constrict. What would he say if she told him the truth? That she loved him. It was not something she could think about with any degree of composure. Already her heart was thumping heavily, her eyes glittering with unshed tears.

'Well, Lee?' Gilles taunted. 'Can a woman love the man who takes her without pity or compunction, purely to satisfy his own desires?'

He was gone before she could reply, leaving her to finish dressing in a hazy blur of mingled pain and anguish.

CHAPTER SEVEN

Now at last she could begin to relax, Lee thought, expelling her breath slightly.

Throughout the meal she had been on tenterhooks lest anything go wrong, but to judge from the relaxed hum of conversation all around her, their guests had thoroughly enjoyed their meal. At the far end of the table, Gilles' dark head was turned towards one of their guests, and she could observe him without him being aware of it. In the uniform of Napoleon's hussars he looked so magnificently male that her treacherous heart had trembled with aching desire for his love. Her fingers crept to the pearls encircling her throat. Gilles had placed them there before dinner. When he left their room she had thought he would not return, but he did, carrying the small, flat jeweller's box which had held the pearls René de Chauvigny had given to his bride.

'My ancestress would have it that René gave her these as a symbol of his own tears, cried when he realised how much he had harmed her.'

'But you can't mean me to wear them,' Lee had protested.

'Why not? You are my wife. It is expected that you should have some jewellery besides your rings.'

Mention of these reminded Lee of Drew's diamond, which still had to be returned to him, and she had asked Gilles to give it to her.

'Why?' he had demanded coldly. 'You cannot wear it.'

She could not explain to him that she had wanted to send the ring back to Drew, she thought on a sigh. The man seated to her left had drunk deeply of Gilles' wine and Lee had already had to remove his clammy hand from her thigh twice. He had come alone and she remembered Gilles telling her that he was recently divorced. Lee did not care for him very much, and she was glad to be able to escape to the drawing room.

Louise had come dressed as Josephine. She had waylaid Gilles by the door, fluttering her ostrich fan provocatively as she slid her fingers along his arm.

'That one has no self-respect,' Madame Lefleur commented critically. 'She thinks only of appeasing her own desires. Gilles had a fortunate escape.'

'She is very beautiful,' Lee commented unthinkingly.

Her companion's eyes widened. 'Surely you are not jealous of her? Why, it is obvious that Gilles feels nothing but disgust for her. Why do you not tell him about the baby?' she said softly. 'You cannot doubt that he will be pleased.'

Couldn't she? If she was the pure, unsullied bride of impeccable family whom he had wanted, *then* no doubt he would have been pleased. But she wasn't. She was just the girl he had married... Her heart jerked suddenly as though it were on strings. She *was* the girl he had married, and if her child was a son, in law it would stand to inherit Gilles' title and possessions. She glanced fearfully at her husband, still talking to Louise, his expression remote and withdrawn. No, he must not find out about the baby, otherwise he might try and take it from her.

'*Chérie*, are you all right? You look so pale. They are not easy, these first months...'

Madame Lefleur looked so concerned that Lee forced a small smile.

'It's nothing, and I'm very healthy.'

'Well, may I suggest that you rescue your poor husband from Louise before she devours him completely?'

Remembering the state of the guest bedroom, Lee had to stifle a small stab of satisfaction as she saw Louise studying her covertly. Had she hoped to bring Gilles' wrath down upon her head by urging the housekeeper into the wanton act of destruction, or had it been wholly the other woman's idea? Perhaps she would never know.

'Louise.' Lee smiled coolly at her, her own fingers touching Gilles' arm lightly as she drew his attention away from the redhead and to herself.

'It is time for us to open the ball.'

Whatever else one might say about Gilles, she could not deny that he was a first-rate actor, Lee thought bitterly. His smile for her was slow and sensual, the touch of his lips against her fingers as he lifted them to his mouth and brushed them lightly that of a possessive lover. Louise glared at them, her lips thinning slightly as she looked assessingly at Lee.

'You are putting on weight, *chérie*,' she said spitefully. 'You will have to be careful,' she warned Gilles, 'otherwise you will have a dumpy wife, *mon ami*.'

'Dumpy?' To Lee's astonishment Gilles' eyebrows rose mockingly, his voice a soft purr as he murmured seductively, 'Oh come, Louise, you exaggerate. As Lee's husband, I can assure you that there is nothing about her body that does not give me the utmost delight.'

Several people had overheard them and turned to smile at Lee, who felt hot colour suffusing her cheeks.

'How would you say that!' she protested as Gilles placed her arm through his and led her on to the newly polished parquet floor.

The musicians struck up a waltz and Lee was swung round to face the cool grey eyes, Gilles' arm resting determinedly against her waist.

'What would you have had me say?' he enquired in bored accents. 'That I did not feel the least desire for you? My dear Lee,' he told her dryly, 'our guests are sophisticated men and women of the world, they would not have believed me for a second.'

'Then what will you tell them when I'm gone?' she asked bitterly.

'We will not speak of this now.' He was angry and Lee quivered in his arms. 'Oh, for God's sake,' he demanded harshly, 'what do you think I'm going to do to you? Ravish you in front of all our guests?'

The music stopped and suddenly Lee was set free. She could see Gilles' dark blue-coated back disappearing as he mingled with the other costumed dancers and her eyes grew dark with pain. A passing waiter hovered with a tray of fluted champagne glasses. So great had been Lee's desire to repeat that earlier ball in every detail that even this touch had been faithfully reproduced, and she drank the sparkling liquid with a recklessness which was totally out of character. She didn't care, she told herself as she consumed her second glass. She didn't care what happened. Gilles was dancing with Louise and her eyes seemed to devour him. The woman was repellent, Lee thought with a shudder, unaware of how young and innocent she herself looked in her pale green gown, her hair caught up to reveal the tender nape of her neck.

'Dance with me, sweet seductress?'

It was the man who had been seated next to her at dinner, and unwillingly Lee agreed. He held her too tightly, his hot breath fanning her face.

'Gilles is a lucky devil to have a bride like you. So innocent in looks—and yet if I know Gilles he will have lost no time in initiating you into the ways of love. But now he seeks fresh pastures with Madame Louise, but you and I will comfort one another.'

Before Lee could stop him he had manoeuvred her out on to one of the small wrought iron balconies overlooking the gardens, and although she protested hotly, she was not strong enough to prevent him from raining moist, loathsome kisses on her exposed shoulders and face.

His hand was reaching towards her breast, and Lee clawed desperately to be free, falling back against the balcony, when he was suddenly pulled away from her and she was blessedly free of this unpleasant embrace.

'A thousand pardons, Gilles,' her attacker muttered thickly. 'Your wine…the loveliness of your wife…'

'And what is your excuse?' Gilles demanded coldly when the other man had hurried away.

Lee's eyes widened angrily.

'My *excuse*? You surely can't have thought that I wanted him to kiss me?'

'You didn't seem to be doing much objecting from where I was standing.'

Lee shivered, suddenly cold.

'You've already made one false assumption about me, Gilles,' she reminded him quietly. 'Don't make any more.'

'I wondered when you were going to throw that in my face.' His savagery seemed to reach out and hold her prisoner on the small balcony. 'You gave yourself to me willingly enough, for all that you were a virgin.' His mouth twisted bitterly. 'What am I supposed to think? I know too well the torment of unquenched desire, the need to slake it, no matter what the cost.' His voice had dropped; he was almost talking to himself. Lee went white and clutched at the supporting rail behind her. Was that how it had been for him with her? A desire which had to be slaked no matter what amount of self-loathing might follow?

'No!' The anguished cry burst past her lips and she took one unsteady step forward followed by another,

intent only on seeking the privacy of her room to hide
from Gilles before he forced her to admit the truth,
but a strange grey mist seemed to be reaching out for
her, all round her anxious voices, and then nothing
but a sensation of falling…falling endlessly, until her
downward sweep was stopped by something hard and
warm.

'ARE YOU FEELING better now, *chérie*?'

The soft, concerned voice was familiar and Lee
struggled to remember why, her forehead puckered in
a frown.

'Madame Lefleur!'

She hadn't realised she had said the name out loud
until her companion smiled. 'Please call me Dominique. You gave us all a fright, fainting like that.'

'Gilles?' Lee lifted her head from the pillow,
astounded to find she was wearing only a flimsy
nightdress.

'He has returned to his guests.'

Of course—the ball! What must everyone think of
her?

I'm afraid your secret is no longer your own,'
Dominique told her, answering her unspoken question. 'Fortunately one of your guests is a doctor and
he was able to soothe all the very natural fears of the
father-to-be.'

When Lee gave a faint, anguished moan, she added
gently, 'I'm afraid you will have some explaining to
do, *chérie*. He hid it well, but he was not pleased, I
think, to discover his paternity in this fashion. Your

guests of course are all enchanted, and Gilles has had to endure much teasing upon the subject of his virility. I shall leave you now,' she said briskly. 'Do not be afraid. Gilles is a just and compassionate man, Lee, I cannot think he would treat you unkindly.'

'But he'll want his child.' Tears rolled down her face, and Dominique stared at her, frowning.

'Of a surety, *petite*.' Her brow cleared and for the first time she looked severe. 'You were not planning to deprive him of it? That would be unfair, and somehow I think not like you. I shall leave you to sleep and perhaps think on the advantages to your child of having both parents to watch over it.'

Sleep had never been farther away. The night was warm, balmy almost, and Lee curled up in a chair beside the window, watching the moonlight play on the still waters of the moat. How different things would be if Gilles really loved her, if this child was really wanted. There were sounds of activity in the courtyard, cheery 'goodnights' and car engines starting. Wrapped in her own thoughts, Lee was barely aware of the bedroom door opening and of Gilles surveying her fragile body, her head resting on the knees she had pulled up to her chin. He moved and she turned, her eyes widening, mirroring her fear. Without a word Gilles closed the door. Tonight he looked older, and Lee trembled as he came towards her.

Sitting down made her feel at a disadvantage and she scrambled to her feet, remembering too late the sheer nightdress.

Gilles drew in a sharp breath and mirrored in the

window Lee saw her own reflection and knew the reason for it. Without the cloak of her clothes the slight swell of her stomach was clearly visible, as was the heavy ripeness of her breasts, and as though aware of the import of the moment the new life inside her fluttered and kicked, the tiny movement suspending her breath.

'So it is true.' The harsh words brought her back to reality, her hands going instinctively to her stomach.

'No! Let me look at you.' Her hands were wrenched away as Gilles' eyes travelled the length of her body.

'My child,' he said thickly at last, 'and you weren't even going to tell me. No wonder you were so anxious to leave here! What were you going to do? A discreet operation? Or has it gone too far for that? An orphanage perhaps, or did you hope to persuade your Brahmin to accept it into his family?'

Before Lee could stop him the nightdress had been torn from her with a rage that Gilles was making no attempt to hide, and she shrank back as he reached for her. His hands were surprisingly gentle, touching the changed contours of her body, in a manner which in another man would be almost reverent. Lee trembled as he spread his fingers over the gentle swell of her womb.

'You will not harm my child,' he told her huskily, 'if I have to watch over you night and day to make sure you don't.'

Lee had expected him to want the child once it was

born, but this emotion—this was something she had not visualised.

'I had no intention of harming the baby,' she told him angrily. 'What sort of woman do you think I am, Gilles? But I still want my freedom,' she told him bravely.

'No!' His hands tightened and Lee gasped as she felt the child kick protestingly. Gilles released her. 'What...?'

'That was your son, or daughter,' she told him lightly. He had gone very pale, and she had the ridiculous urge to comfort him, because it was plain that he thought he had hurt her. 'He or she doesn't like being squeezed so hard.'

'You mean...' His eyes had fastened on her body, and Lee smiled, surprised to find herself so free of embarrassment, so almost maternal.

'Babies don't just lie there and do nothing,' she told him teasingly, 'They kick. And this one kicks very hard!'

All at once she felt very tired. The evening had been a long one.

'The dinner... Everything went well, I hope?' she asked sleepily, walking towards the bed. 'The buyers...'

'Were full of compliments,' Gilles told her absently. 'Lee, this...this child changes everything. You realise if it is a boy he will be my heir?'

'Yes!' Her heart seemed to be being squeezed in some giant vice.

'Our marriage must continue, Lee,' Gilles told her

in a hard voice. 'You must realise this?' His eyes darkened suddenly. '*Parbleu*, I have it! You knew what I would say and this was why you kept your condition secret from me!'

'You were the one who said that marriage and children were a serious matter,' Lee reminded him. 'All I want for my child is love, Gilles, not position or possessions, just love.'

There was a strange look on his face, almost darkly brooding as he turned to watch her his fingers once more tracing the outline of her stomach.

'And you think I will not give him that?' His voice was oddly low. He bent suddenly and touched his lips to her burgeoning flesh. 'On the contrary,' he muttered huskily, tracing her rounded outline with soft kisses.

His touch seemed to ignite her flesh, and flames of desire burned through her, compelling her to reach out and run trembling fingers through the night-darkness of his hair, pressing him closer to her body.

'What the hell are you doing to me, Lee?' he groaned thickly. 'Don't you know what it's doing to me, seeing you like this? My child growing inside you?'

Lee didn't reply. She could not. Was he saying that he found her pregnancy exciting? That he desired her? A terrible weakness invaded her body. Common sense told her to resist him, but how could she heed common sense when Gilles was lifting her in his arms, carrying her gently to the bed, and placing her gently on it while slowly and deliberately he began to arouse her yielding flesh.

This time there was no heated urgency, no fierce demanding clamour for appeasement. This time she was floating on a warm buoyant sea. But all seas have tides, and soon she felt the insistent pull of hers, her fingers stroking the hard warmth of Gilles' shoulders, burrowing in the hair shadowing his chest.

'Lee,' he groaned protestingly, when she touched his stomach, so lean and flat. His breath was warm against her breasts, tender now and acutely sensitive to his touch.

He was gentle with her, almost tender, and yet still arousing her to a point where nothing mattered save that he possess her, completely and absolutely, and although she was too proud to tell him so herself, her body did it for her, her response as deeply passionate as it had been that first time, only now the pleasure was prolonged, drawn out until she thought she would die from it.

'There is no going back now, Lee,' Gilles told her softly as she slid into sleep, 'so you had best make up your mind to admit that you do desire me.'

'Even though there's no love?'

The words slipped out drowsily, threaded with pain.

'There is love,' Gilles told her in a deep voice. 'For the life we have created together.'

And as she fell asleep Lee's last thoughts were envious ones of her child, who already possessed what Gilles would never give her—his love.

THE MOMENT SHE woke up Lee knew that something
was different. For a start, she was not alone in the
bed. And then the memory came flooding back, and
she turned her head and saw Gilles lying at her side,
his hair tousled with sleep, a dark shadow lying along
his jaw. In sleep he looked curiously vulnerable. Sup-
pressing a desire to touch him, she slid out of the bed,
padding round the room quietly as she collected her
clothes and headed for the bathroom.

The sting of the water did much to dissipate the
feeling of languor with which she had awoken and
she lingered longer than usual under the shower.
Against her will her eyes were drawn to her body.

'Is it your condition that disgusts you, or the fact
that it's my child?'

The harsh words held her motionless and she stared
at Gilles, shock sending the blood drumming through
her veins as her eyes slid feverishly over his naked
body.

His eyes began to darken as he stared at her damp
body, and Lee knew from the pulsating response he
evoked within her that he wanted her.

'No!' Her moaned protest was ignored. She re-
treated into the shower, thinking that Gilles would
never follow her into the small enclosed space, but
he did, reaching for her with a hunger that surprised
her. She knew that men could feel desire without
love, but the intensity of Gilles'—especially after last
night—puzzled her. It was as though what had happened then had merely been an appetiser before the
main meal.

'Don't tell me you don't want me, Lee,' he ordered thickly as she tried to escape him. 'And don't tell me you're not going to let me make love to you, when every movement of your body urges me to possess you.'

'Make love?' Lee demanded hysterically, seizing on the two words which had caused her the most pain. 'How can you call it that?' Tears blurred her vision, but she could feel the heat of Gilles' anger. His hands slid over her back, moulding her against him, letting her know that she had aroused him.

'I don't want you!' She knew the words were a lie, but somehow she had to hold on to her sanity, to prevent herself from being sucked down into the quagmire of passion that would leave her physically fulfilled but mentally aching for something more than mere sexual satisfaction.

'You don't?' His voice held silky enquiry, but he released her quite readily, watching her as she reached for a towel.

She left him in the bathroom, wishing she had some means of locking him in while she finished dressing. Although he had released her, passion has still smouldered deep in his eyes. Louise had already hinted that she would find it difficult to satisfy his sensual appetite, and now Lee was beginning to think she had been right. Before, when their marriage was only to be temporary, he had held aloof, no doubt not wanting the complications that a sexual relationship could bring, but now, with her carrying his child and their marriage permanent, it was obvious that he had cyn-

ically decided that she could take over Louise's role.
Well, she would not! Her fingers trembled as she
dried herself quickly. Keeping one eye on the bathroom door, she searched feverishly for the oil she was
using on her tenderly stretched skin. Busily engrossed
in this task, she wasn't aware of Gilles standing behind her until she felt his breath stir her hair. She
moved forward, but she was not quick enough; Gilles'
arms imprisoned her, his chest hard and warm against
her back.

'What are you doing?' His eyes lingered on the
satin gleam of her skin, and looking down at her own
body, Lee acknowledged with a heavily thumping
heart that her actions might unknowingly have
seemed provocative to an onlooker. Even so her
cheeks burned. If they were to stay married she would
demand separate rooms. She could not endure this
intimacy for much longer, even though the thought of
its cessation made her ache slightly inside.

'It's to prevent stretch marks,' she explained nervously, reaching for the bottle. 'Gilles, I should like
my own room,' she added.

'Why?' His eyes were fastened on her body and
she licked her lips nervously. 'You do not wish me
to watch my child growing inside you?'

His words touched her with the knowledge that she
did. To hide her reaction she said lightly, 'Many men
find the sight of pregnant women unpleasant.'

'And you wish to save me from this unpleasantness?' His tone told her that he did not believe her,
and to Lee's dismay he removed the bottle she had

been holding and uncapping it poured some of the clear liquid into his palm, and holding her imprisoned against him with one hand, began slowly to massage the taut skin of her stomach with the other.

'I do not find the sight of you swelling with my child unpleasant, Lee,' he told her harshly. 'On the contrary, I find it unbearably erotic.' His hands cupped her breasts, the warm contact with his skin hardening her nipples immediately. 'Like the grapes your skin has taken on a new bloom.' He was smoothing the oil rhythmically into her body and Lee felt herself melting helplessly beneath his arousing touch. She wanted to protest that he had no right to touch her like this, but every nerve end was quivering in heated response to him. 'They always say that morning is the best time to make love,' he muttered hoarsely as he stopped caressing her and picked her up. 'Hate me all you like, Lee, but you can't deny you want me.'

It was true, she could not. Tears stood out in her eyes as she stared helplessly at the dark head fastened against her breast. There was something almost obsessive about his desire for her, something that reached out into the innermost recesses of her own soul, and yet terrified her in its intensity.

'It's obscene!' she protested hysterically. 'You're degrading me!'

His hands stilled and she was jolted upright to stare into furious grey eyes.

'My God!' he breathed angrily. 'I've a good mind to teach you exactly what that word means!'

Beyond reasoning Lee lashed back bitterly, 'You already have! You accuse me of lax morals and worse, impregnate me with your child, use me to slake your desire... What else could there be?'

'This!' he ground out between clenched teeth, forcing her mouth to part in a kiss that humiliated her with its ice-cold contempt, lacerating her soft flesh, and stifling her small pained moans. Even then Lee could not believe that he meant to take her; her mind could simply not comprehend that any man could use such savagery against a woman, but she was soon disabused of this foolish notion.

'The baby!' she moaned protestingly at one point, terrified by the violence she glimpsed in Gilles' face. His bitter laugh jarred on her raw nerves.

'He's safe enough, madame wife. You had the option of admitting that I could arouse you, that you felt desire, but you chose to deny it, to make me lower than a farmyard animal, intent only on slaking a primitive physical urge, and rather than disappoint you, that is exactly what I shall do.'

It was a lesson she would never forget, Lee thought hours later, aching and exhausted, unable to cry, unable to do anything but curse the day she had come to the château de Chauvigny. Her body was bruised from the cold brutality of Gilles' hands, and it seemed impossible to believe that the man who had possessed her with such savage implacability was the same one who had touched her with such tender reverence the night before.

That she was in part to blame she could not deny.

Calling his touch degrading had seemed to unleash in Gilles a rage she had never dreamed he possessed. She would have to get up. It must be nearly lunchtime and heaven knew what excuses Gilles had made to their guests. Most of them were leaving after breakfast, and Lee only hoped that by the time she got downstairs they would all have gone. Her wan face and bruised eyes told their own story. Her skin had a bloom, he had told her, and he had crushed it carelessly underfoot, destroying it for ever. She shivered, despite the warmth of the room. From now on she would sleep in the tower room and Gilles could protest as much as he liked. If he wanted to slake his desires in future he could do so with someone else! All the love she had felt for him had been crushed and destroyed—or so she told herself as she dressed slowly, trying to instill some sort of urgency into her aching limbs.

CHAPTER EIGHT

'Now you hold the baby, Lee,' Marie-Thérèse pleaded. 'I want a photograph of you with her—and you too, Gilles. Put your arm round Lee,' she instructed. 'That's better.'

Lee went taut the moment Gilles placed his hand on her waist. They were standing outside the small Norman church in Chauvigny and the sun was shining mellowly on the ancient stones. Lee had been astonished and flattered when Marie-Thérèse and Jean-Paul had asked Gilles and herself to stand as godparents to little Claire-Jeanne, and now, holding the baby in her beautifully embroidered christening gown, Lee tried to dismiss the wave of anguish threatening to engulf her. In three months her own child would be born, and the trap which her marriage to Gilles had turned into would completely enclose her.

As she handed the small, warm bundle back to Marie-Thérèse, she smiled at the other girl. Motherhood had brought a soft bloom to her cheeks and no one looking at the small family could doubt their happiness. All the guests had been invited back to the house after the christening. Lee had spent most of the morning helping Marie-Thérèse to prepared a cold buffet, and as Gilles helped her into the car she glanced covertly at his set profile.

Since the night of the ball he had grown into a distant stranger. They still shared a room—he had insisted on that—but for all the time they were together in it they need not have done. His manner towards her was cold and remote. When he saw her he asked conscientiously after her health, and she responded in a similarly polite fashion, neither of them in any doubt that their marriage was a hell which had to be endured for the sake of their child.

'Are you all right?' She hadn't realised that he was watching her. 'You look tired,' he added abruptly. 'You mustn't do too much.'

'I'm fine.' Physically perhaps, but mentally she was not. On her last visit to the doctor he had commented in a puzzled fashion on her frail wrists and slender legs and had told her to eat plenty of good country food. It would take more than food to tempt her waning appetite, Lee admitted wryly; it would take something she was never likely to have, her husband's love. Tears blurred her eyes as she remembered how tenderly Jean-Paul had looked at his wife and child, and as she looked into Gilles' shuttered face she felt as though a door had been slammed in her face, and all her chances of happiness locked away behind it.

Louise and her father had attended the christening and were at the house when Gilles and Lee arrived.

'I have not yet congratulated you, Gilles,' Monsieur Trouville commented, with a smile. 'I have been

telling Louise that it is time she remarried and pro-
vided me with some grandchildren.'

'Children!' Louise shuddered delicately, her eyes
on Lee's body. 'They ruin your figure. No, Papa. It
is a wife's duty to provide her husband with a son,
of course, but these women who devote themselves
to the upbringing of their children become so boring.
Do you not find it so, Gilles?'

Thus appealed to, Gilles smiled. 'Certainly no one
could imagine you becoming boring, Louise,' was his
only comment. Nothing more was said, but Lee knew
that Louise was subtly reminding him of all that he
had given up, and perhaps that it was still there waiting for him, should he choose to take it.

'You must rest, *chérie*,' Marie-Thérèse ordered
Lee. 'You look pale, and Gilles would never forgive
me if you were to overtire yourself. You are all ready
for the *bébé*, *non*?'

Lee shook her head. She had made no preparations
for the arrival of the child, somehow hoping that by
doing so she was leaving herself the option of escaping from the château and the unhappiness it held, but
deep down inside she knew that this was impossible.
Gilles would never allow her to leave, not now.

It was early evening before the party broke up, and
Lee's back was aching from the constant standing.
Marie-Thérèse and Jean-Paul came with them to the
car, Marie-Thérèse frowning a little as she saw her
pale face. She had grown very fond of Lee, but her
feminine instincts told her that all was not well with

her new friend, and they were not close enough for her to ask what was wrong.

'You must look after Lee, Gilles,' she instructed as Gilles opened the car door. 'She does not look well. It is a difficult time for a woman, especially when she is far from her family.'

Gilles turned and looked at her, and for a moment Lee thought she glimpsed bitterness in the steel grey eyes. Was he perhaps feeling resentment that he too was trapped in this travesty of a marriage?

'Is that true, *chérie*?' he asked softly, his fingers stroking her cheek gently. The imitation tenderness was for the benefit of his friends, Lee knew, but it was impossible to prevent herself from responding to his touch, her colour coming and going swiftly, as just for a moment she closed her eyes to the truth and let herself believe that *this* was real—the warmth of his fingers against her skin, the look in his eyes as he smiled down at her, the warmth of his body as he pulled her gently against him, his lips resting lightly on her temple. Lee let herself absorb his strength, giving in to the irresistible urge to close her eyes and relax against his hard chest.

'Lee?' There was sharp anxiety in the word, and his arm came tightly round her, his fingers under her chin forcing her face upwards so that her eyes opened reluctantly, her heart warmed by his sudden urgency.

'*Are* you feeling ill? The baby…?'

Her heart plummeted. Of course—his concern was all for his child, not for her.

'I'm just tired.' She pulled away from him, not

wanting him to see the betraying sparkle of tears, not wanting the others to guess how much she had longed to prolong the physical contact that Gilles seemed only too anxious to bring to an end.

'Tomorrow I am going into Nantes,' Gilles announced abruptly as they drove away. 'I have some business there. You will need things for the baby. Would you like to come with me, or shall I send to Paris?'

'You won't mind?'

You won't mind having me with you, was what she had meant, but Gilles frowned. 'It makes no difference to me, I merely thought that you would wish to choose the things yourself. However, I do realise that my child can't be expected to arouse the same maternal delight in your breast that your ex-fiancé's might have done.' His voice had grown very hard during this speech, and for a moment Lee was tempted to tell him just how she felt about his child, but to do so would be to give herself away completely, and their relationship was already fraught with sufficient hazards without her adding the burden of her love to them.

'I should like to come with you,' she said quietly. 'I only meant that I might be in the way.'

'If that were the case I wouldn't ask you to come with me.'

He said nothing further and Lee sensed that the subject was closed. When they reached the château he disappeared in the direction of the cellars. The new wine was due to be racked off, and Lee knew that he would want to supervise this personally. She was feeling too tired to face a meal alone in the huge dining room, and instead asked for a tray to be brought to the bedroom.

One of the young maids brought it, staring round-eyed round the luxurious bedroom before placing the appetising tray on a small table.

There was some chicken and home-cured ham with a crisp green salad, and fresh strawberries with cream for dessert. Lee knew she ought to feel hungry, but she could only stare at the food apathetically. She knew what was wrong with her; she was sickening for Gilles' love. She pushed the table away and read the letter she had received from her parents that morning once more.

The news of her marriage had surprised and delighted them, and her mother had written that they hoped to fly to France after the baby's birth to see them all. She had never been particularly drawn to Drew, Lee's mother wrote, surprising Lee by adding that she had sensed in her daughter a deeply passionate nature which would not have found contentment with a man of Drew's essentially cold temperament.

That might have been so, but at least she would not have known the aching agony she was enduring now, longing for the impossible.

She was asleep when Gilles came in and not able to witness the look in his eyes as he glanced from her sleeping body to the uneaten food, his face taut with an emotion which could have been anger.

To Lee's surprise she found Gilles downstairs in

the small sitting room where she normally had breakfast, and then she remembered that they were going
to Nantes.

'They are bringing some fresh croissants,' he informed her, pulling out her chair. 'I have already
eaten.'

'Oh, I don't want anything,' Lee started to protest,
but Gilles swept her objections aside, practically
standing over her while she ate two of the deliciously
warm, flaky rolls spread with apricot conserve. To
Lee's own surprise she quite enjoyed them, but then
she did not normally have the presence of her husband at breakfast, and as Gilles poured them both a
second cup of coffee, she admitted that this might
have something to do with her improved appetite.

She put down her large coffee cup to find Gilles
watching her. The cup was heavy and she had been
holding it with both hands, breathing in the fragrance
of the coffee.

'You look like a little girl,' he said sardonically.

'But I'm not. I'm a woman of twenty-two.'

A shadow seemed to pass over his face, but before
Lee could question it he was standing up, muscles
rippling under the knitted cotton shirt which bared his
tanned forearms with their sprinkling of dark hairs.

He looked exactly what he was, she thought as he
opened the door for her—a sensual, sophisticated
man, impervious to the uncertainties which beset
lesser mortals.

Nantes was a bustling city, far larger than Lee had
imagined, and she was just beginning to wonder how

she was going to manage not to lose herself when Gilles surprised her by announcing that he would accompany her while she did her shopping.

'But your business…'

'A visit to a wine shipper which will take no more than half an hour at the most. We shall go there after lunch. If I do not come with you, you will tire yourself out doing far too much. You seem to forget that you are with child. Or is it that you wish you could forget?'

'I wish I could forget everything!' Lee burst out, very close to tears. It was ridiculous, but she was growing jealous of her own child; jealous of Gilles' care and concern for it, when he made no attempt to conceal his contempt of her. 'I wish I'd never come to Chauvigny; never allowed myself to be blackmailed into this farce of a marriage; and most of all never conceived your child!'

She watched Gilles turn white and would have walked away from him, driven to escape the fury in his eyes, if he had not had hold of her wrist.

'You listen to me!' he told her through gritted teeth. 'Hate me as much as you wish, Lee, but the child is innocent of any crime, and you will never, never allow it to know that it was ever resented by its mother.'

'A mother whom its father despises,' Lee reminded him bitterly. 'Gilles, let me go home. Divorce me…'

'And allow my child to be brought up by another? Never!'

Lee knew that for her own sanity she ought to consider giving up the child into Gilles' custody, but merely to contemplate such an action caused her the most acute pain. Just as Gilles would not allow his child to grow up away from Chauvigny, neither could she give it up to the woman Gilles would marry in her place—a woman who could never love either of them as much as she did.

In a hostile silence Gilles directed her towards an exclusive arcade of shops.

In one of them Lee pored over beautiful coach-built prams and broderie anglaise-festooned cribs, all so expensive that she turned regretfully from them to more practical items, but to her surprise Gilles lingered, drawing her attention to a delightful cradle that rocked gently when touched.

'The baby would grow out of it very quickly,' Lee commented regretfully, but to her surprise, instead of turning away, Gilles said to the saleswoman, 'My wife likes it, although her puritan English streak will not permit her to say so. We will take it. The baby may quickly outgrow it, but there will be others.'

Lee had picked up enough French to follow the conversation, and her eyes widened at this blatant untruth. Gilles had adopted a personality she barely recognised. The nursery was going to be the most lavishly equipped she had ever seen, and eventually, when the saleswoman's arms were full of fluffy toys of all descriptions, Lee took a back seat and let Gilles get on with it.

'They are always like this with the first,' the

woman told Lee with a smile, 'these proud, doting papas.'

Gilles, proud? Doting? Lee took another look at him. He seemed to be enjoying himself hugely.

'We shan't need that!' she gasped when he insisted on ordering a luxurious coach-built pram.

'You will want to take him for walks when it is fine,' Gilles argued. 'And this pram will be easier to push.'

It was two hours before they left the shop. When they stepped out into the autumn sunshine, Gilles cupped a hand under Lee's elbow. Lee saw their reflections in a shop window—Gilles tall and protective, herself smaller, frailer.

'Lee, I propose that we call a truce. I cannot put aside our marriage, but I give you my word that there will be no repetitions of the events which led to our present *impasse*.'

'And what does that mean? That you're condemning us both to a life of celibacy? Or that you'll resume your relationship with Louise, safe in the knowledge that she can no longer force you into marriage?'

Lee had never seen him so angry, and if she had not been so bitterly hurt by what he had said she doubted that she would ever have dared to speak so forcefully.

He swore angrily, pulling her into a shadowed arcade so that they could not be overheard.

'Enough! You are determined to believe the worst of me! All I was trying to do was to assure you that you need not freeze like a glacier every time I come near you. You are not eating. You look pale and ill…'

'And you think that telling me I needn't fear your…your unwanted attention is going to change all that?' Lee was close to hysteria. 'You're condemning me to a life without love, to a marriage which is a meaningless farce…'

'And what the hell am I supposed to do?' Gilles was equally angry now. 'Let you bring up my son on your own, for that Brahmin will not marry you now…'

'I wish to God I wasn't having your child, then I could be free…'

The moment she uttered them Lee knew the words to be false. She didn't want to be free; and anyway she never could. What she wanted was for Gilles to love her with the depth and intensity of her love for him.

Gilles had gone completely silent, his eyes like ice.

'Only this morning you told me that you were a woman, Lee. You lied. You're still a selfish, unseeing child.'

'Where are you taking me?'

He was propelling her along the pavement and she tried to hang back, reluctant to go with him.

'To lunch. I've already booked the table.'

'I'm not hungry.' Lee knew that she was being childish, and regretted the words when Gilles turned to stare coolly at her, before saying,

'Perhaps not, but you will eat. If you behave like a child, Lee, then you must expect to be treated as such. What are you trying to do?' he demanded harshly. 'Starve the child to death? Destroy it before it is even born?'

Lee went white, swaying slightly as she stared up at him. 'That's a hateful thing to say!'

'No more "hateful" than what you said yourself a few moments ago, but you will not have your freedom at the price of the baby's life, Lee, and if you were truly a woman you would not want it.'

There was nothing she could say. Those bitter, wild words had been born of her own aching need to be wanted for herself, but she could hardly explain that without betraying her love. If she was to survive this marriage she must learn to be as distant and clinical as Gilles, but how could she achieve that when every time she saw him she yearned to touch him, when even the sound of his voice made her melt with longing, and even in her dreams the memories of his love-making pursued her relentlessly?

THE RESTAURANT WAS in a luxurious new hotel block. The head waiter murmured something to Gilles, whom he quite obviously knew, and then Lee felt Gilles' hand on her arm as he guided her across acres of thick pile carpet to a table by the window where two people were already sitting.

The words, 'What are Michael and Anna doing here?' were trembling on her lips, but before she could utter them Michael was standing up, beaming down at her, and claiming the privilege of a friend by kissing her cheek.

'Surprise, surprise!' Anna said gaily when they were all sitting down. 'I was so intrigued by all that Michael told me about the Loire that we decided to spend our holiday here. We're only in Nantes for the one night, and when Michael rang the château to see if it was convenient to come and see you, I was thrilled when Gilles suggested we lunch together.'

Lee liked Anna and had always got on well with her, but for once she found conversation difficult. Gilles had said nothing to her about Michael's telephone call. Why had he not invited them to the château?

As though he had read her mind, Gilles broke off his conversation with Michael to say urbanely to Lee, '*Now* you know why I wanted you to come to Nantes with me. I didn't want to spoil the surprise by telling you beforehand. At one time I thought I was going to have to use force,' he joked with Michael, who was smiling at Lee. 'I've never known a woman so reluctant to spend her husband's money!'

Naturally Michael and Anna laughed, while Lee bent her head over the table. Gilles had arranged this lunch as a surprise for her? She could not think why, unless it was to reinforce his determination to make their marriage permanent. Perhaps he had wanted to bring home to her the fact that her friends already believed in the myth!

'We've spent the morning equipping the nursery,' Gilles added, further confounding Lee, who flushed a little under Michael's quizzical smile, and Anna was immediately nostalgic about her own pregnancies, and their children, who were now almost grown up.

'Do you remember, Michael?' she asked her husband. 'When James was born you were in Scotland. He arrived two weeks early,' she explained to Lee, 'and I was all on my own. My parents were on holiday, and Michael's mother was staying with his sister.'

'And I've never been allowed to forget my error,' said Michael ruefully, but still smiling. It was impossible for Lee to envisage Gilles and herself in middle age with many years of marriage behind them, teasing one another about their shared past, and all at once tears blurred her eyes, the delicious fish she had been eating almost choking her as misery tightened her throat. She was glad that the others were too engrossed in their conversation to be aware of her own silence, and it wasn't until she felt Gilles' fingers on her wrist that she realised he was aware of her distress.

'I thought the sight of your friends would please you,' he told her in a low undertone, when Michael and Anna's attention was elsewhere. 'But instead you sulk like a spoiled child!'

It was impossible for Lee to explain that she wasn't sulking; and nearly as impossible for her to comprehend that this lunch had been arranged purely for her pleasure. She shot a look at Gilles. In fact she did not believe it. Why would he do anything to make her happy? Far more likely that he was thinking of his child's wellbeing!

IT WAS A LITTLE after three o'clock when they left the restaurant, having said goodbye to Michael and Anna, who were leaving Nantes that afternoon. Lee was surprised to find that Gilles expected her to join him in the office of the wine shipper, who expressed deferential interest when Gilles informed him of Lee's training and career.

'But that of course is now all at an end,' the shipper commented. 'As Madame la Comtesse…'

'As Madam la Comtesse,' Gilles interrupted firmly, much to Lee's astonishment, 'my wife will naturally take her place at my side, running the château and the business. Why else do you think I married her?' he teased, smiling at Lee. 'She is going to be a considerable asset.'

On the way back to the car Lee asked hesitantly, 'Did you mean that, Gilles? About me helping you in the business, I mean?'

'Would you want to?' His eyes surveyed her, the dark head inclined politely, and her heart melted with love. 'It would mean that on occasions we would have to work closely together.' They had reached the car and he bent to unlock the door. 'Would you want that?'

Would she? Would she want the torture of his constant presence and constant unavailability?

'Your eyes give you away,' Gilles said harshly before she could reply, helping her into her seat. He leaned across to check that her door was closed securely, his bare arm brushing against her breasts. Her response was immediate and she flushed hotly, sure that he must have felt her betraying tremble.

Today had been full of surprises, and all at once she wanted to believe that Gilles had arranged the lunch with Michael and Anna for her; that he did want her working alongside him; that he did want... Here she stopped her wayward thoughts, saying instead the first thing that came into her mind,

'Do we have time to go to Chinon on the way back?' she asked him. She had always had a keen interest in history and a special fascination for the Plantagenets, whose castle Chinon was.

Gilles' expression was openly sardonic. 'My, my, you are growing brave if you're willing to extend your ordeal and spend further time in my company!'

Lee said nothing, too hurt by his bitter mockery to comment, and as they drove back along the road skirting the Loire she closed her eyes and leaned back in her seat. Gilles slipped a cassette into the car's hi-fi system and the sound of the Carpenters filled the silence. The day had taken its toll of her emotions and as the dying sun warmed the tinted car windows Lee slid softly into sleep.

When she opened her eyes for a moment she didn't know where she was. It was dusk and in the half light she could just make out the vague, shadowy outlines of the castle walls of Chinon. She felt warm and drowsy, and it several seconds before she realised that she was leaning against Gilles, her head pillowed against his shoulder, his arm resting lightly on her waist.

'It seemed a pity to wake you,' was all he said as he removed his arm and allowed her to sit upright.

To conceal the sense of loss brought on by the removal of his body heat Lee searched the darkness outside.

'We could walk round if you wish, although I'm afraid it's too dark to see much.'

He was right, and yet even looking at the remains of this once great fortress made the past come poignantly alive for Lee. Had Berengaria, the lovely but unloved wife of Richard the Lionheart, ever waited within those walls for her husband?

'You look sad.' It was impossible to see Gilles' expression in the gathering darkness, but the words were almost compassionate. 'What were you thinking about?'

'About how arid life is without love to bring it alive,' Lee said truthfully.

'Love? You are clinging to a myth,' Gilles said harshly. 'Your response to me when we made love was unmistakable, Lee, and yet you persist in clinging to your outdated ideology. Do you honestly believe that your Brahmin shares your passionate loyalty?'

Lee turned away. What was the point of dragging Drew into their conversation?

'I'm tired, Gilles,' she told him emotionlessly. 'Please take me home.'

She wasn't aware of having spoken the betraying word, but at her side Gilles stared at her for a moment before starting the car.

'Home? Is that how you view the château, Lee?' he asked softly.

Her cheeks burned and she was glad he could not see the betraying colour.

'I was using the word loosely. What would you prefer me to call it? My prison?'

'You are perfectly free to leave,' Gilles replied equably, 'providing you leave my child behind.'

Lee stared straight ahead of her despite the darkness, her heart filled with bitterness and pain. The night the baby had been conceived was now only a memory, but for the rest of her life she would have to pay and pay again for those moments of shared passion.

LEE PUT DOWN her pen and sealed the envelope with a heartfelt sigh. She would send the letter by registered post, just to be on the safe side. Now that Drew's ring was actually on the way to him, she felt a lot happier. She had told him nothing about the child and could only hope that her mother was right when she said he had a passionless nature. She didn't want to hurt him, and now she could acknowledge that she would never have made him the sort of wife his family would have expected.

Gilles was out, attending a meeting of the local winegrowers' association. The vintage had been a particularly good one. Would Gilles agree to supply Westbury's with some of his lesser quality wines? He had not discussed the matter with her, and she was too proud to ask.

When Madame Le Bon first announced Louise, Lee thought the Frenchwoman must have come to see

Gilles. She was just about to explain that he was not at home, when Louise sank down into one of the antique chairs with fluid grace, stretching out a languid arm for the onyx cigarette lighter and applying the flame to one of the Turkish cigarettes she favoured. Only when she was sure the cigarette was properly lit did she relax back into her chair, her eyes narrowed as she exhaled slowly.

'So…' Her eyes swept Lee's body, and for the first time Lee felt awkwardly ungainly. The redhead was wearing a dress in dark green velvet, the fabric moulding her generous curves. As always her make-up was faultless, and Lee, who had been relaxing in a soft heather-toned pinafore dress over a matching lilac blouse, felt dowdy in comparison.

'You must have succeeded beyond your wildest dreams,' Louise drawled insultingly. 'Oh, come, my dear,' she added when Lee said nothing, 'you surely do not think I was ever taken in by that little charade of Gilles'? A charade which now he is heartily regretting, poor man.' A tinkling laugh assaulted Lee's eardrums. 'But then Gilles always was far too gallant,' Louise continued blithely. 'I remember that summer he spent with his aunt. I warned him that sixteen-year-old girls were apt to be trouble. He did not believe me—then.'

Lee tried not to let her feelings show. Louise was implying that she knew all about that long-ago summer, but surely that could not be true?

'It is true that Gilles wanted to punish me a little and so pretended this long-standing love affair with you, but you cannot have believed he wanted the marriage to be anything other than temporary?'

Delicately arched eyebrows suggested that Lee could surely not have been so stupid as to think that Gilles might have preferred her to Louise.

'Gilles is quite free to divorce me if he wishes,' Lee replied with a calm she was far from feeling. 'That he does not do so must surely tell *you* something, madame.'

For the first time Lee saw the Frenchwoman lose a little of her poise. Her eyes flashed warningly, her hands clenched at her sides. 'So!' she hissed venomously. 'You are not the little innocent we are led to believe. Well, you may have induced Gilles to continue this folly of a marriage, madame, but it will not last. For the moment he is besotted with the idea of this child you carry, but Gilles is a man, with all that the word implies.' She paused delicately, her lips curving in a reminiscent smile. 'Need I say more?'

Lee toyed blindly with the letter in front of her. Louise was right, her words only echoed Lee's own bitter thoughts. Gilles was a man—a man whose potent sexuality would demand an outlet, and who better to provide one than his ex-mistress? There would be no repetition of the events leading to the conception of the child she was carrying, was what he had said, but a man like Gilles could not remain a celibate for ever. Gilles had said nothing about finding Louise unsatisfactory as a mistress; far from it.

'Think about what I have said, *chérie*,' Louise purred, coming across to where Lee was standing, her eyes on the envelope lying on the desk. 'You cannot deceive Gilles for ever. Soon he will discover your hopeless passion for him. That is not what he looks for in a wife,' she added scornfully. 'Or perhaps it is that you hope one day he will come to return your feelings?' She laughed scornfully. 'You silly little English girl with your foolish dreams! Gilles is a Frenchman, a member of the nobility, trained from birth not to expect to find love in his marriage. Leave before it is too late.'

She had reached the door before Lee spoke. Listening to Louise she had run the entire gamut of emotions, but now she knew what she must do. Something in Louise's very evident scorn had awakened her fighting instinct. If she must lose Gilles, then it would not be by default; by running away like a coward and refusing to face up to the truth that Gilles did not love her.

Lifting her head proudly, she smiled at Louise with cool disdain.

'Your concern is most thoughtful, madame,' she replied coolly, 'but quite unnecessary. You see, Gilles already knows that I love him.' Summoning all her acting ability, she permitted herself a small secret smile, touching her stomach lightly. 'And our child is the evidence that he returns my feelings. If you doubt me—ask him.'

She had the satisfaction of seeing Louise's smile freeze into a cold mask. She could only hope the other woman did not call her bluff, Lee thought despairingly, but something in the way she had confronted her with the knowledge of her love had given Lee the idea that Louise was less sure of Gilles than she pretended. Surely if Gilles cared as much for her as she claimed she would have already told him of Lee's feelings?

Ultimately, of course, Lee knew that she could not win, but Louise's threats and malice had sliced through the lethargy which seemed to have possessed her lately. When the Frenchwoman had gone Lee stared out into the empty gardens, now nearly denuded of flowers. Perhaps she could not have Gilles' love, but surely she would win his respect and trust, and who was to say what might not grow from those? They were frail foundations on which to build a future, but they were all she had. Placing Drew's letter in the hall for collection, she made her way upstairs for her afternoon rest, pausing for a moment beneath the portrait of René. A woman had found the key to his heart; if only she could find the key to Gilles'!

'I UNDERSTAND Louise called this afternoon,' Gilles commented abruptly over dinner. 'What did she want?'

'Nothing. It was just a courtesy visit,' Lee lied, wondering what he would say if she told him the truth. She had dressed with special care tonight, wearing one of the new maternity hostess gowns she had ordered from Paris. It was a soft rust velvet with cream collar and cuffs, and with her hair curling down on to her shoulders she had an almost childlike appeal, but when she had glanced in the mirror before coming downstairs she had seen only her bulky shape and awkward movements.

'I have to go to Paris for a few days. Will you be all right?'

Paris? Lee stared at him, her heart thumping heavily. Was this going to be the pattern of their days? Discreet visits to Paris for him while she was left at home?

'Don't you want me to go?'

Lee licked her dry lips. What could she say to that? 'I...'

'If you are worried about the baby—about being alone, I could ask Marie-Thérèse to come and stay with you.'

I want *you*, Lee longed to say. That's all, just you, but of course she could not do that.

'I've been deputised by our local growers' association to talk to the Ministry of Trade about wine exports.'

'And Louise?' The moment the words were out Lee regretted them. She bit her lip in vexation as Gilles frowned sharply.

'What about Louise?'

Lee tried to shrug it off. 'Oh, nothing. I thought perhaps she might be going—I know she spends a lot of time in Paris.' She was babbling like an idiot. Gilles threw down his napkin and walked towards her with purposeful steps. He didn't touch her, but she shrank back in her chair nonetheless, shaken by the depth of the anger in his eyes.

'You thought I was going to Paris with Louise?'

he breathed furiously. 'After all I've told you? My God, that's some imagination you've got there! What the hell... Just what sort of a man do you think I am?'

He was gone before Lee could speak, leaving her alone at the polished mahogany dining table, her face as white as the damask napkin Gilles had thrown down next to a glass of wine the rich, ruby colour of blood.

When she woke up in the morning Gilles had gone, and the tears she had not dared to shed the night before made her throat and eyes ache. She forced herself to get up and go about her normal duties, the whole time her thoughts on Gilles—and how much she loved him.

CHAPTER NINE

LEE glanced out into the courtyard. There had been a sharp frost during the night and the cobblestones were still faintly rimed. Gilles' stallion poked his head over his stable door. No doubt the animal was missing his morning ride. Gilles would not be back for another two days and Lee missed him even though their daily contact was minimal.

After lunch she walked through the gardens. The leaves were already falling, only the clipped yew hedges still green. Autumn was such a sad season, permeated with nostalgia for the dying year. A tide of melancholy swept her as she glanced up at the château walls. If she was not such a coward she would pack her bags and leave, but she could not endure the thought of never seeing Gilles again, even though she knew her love was hopeless.

She paused by the moat watching the swans, too bulky to bend down with any ease. Someone hailed her and she turned, surprised to see Madame Le Bon hurrying towards her across the velvet turf.

She was out of breath when she reached Lee, panting slightly. '*Madam*, it is the wine,' she announced anxiously. 'Pierre wishes to consult with you. He is in the far cellar. I will come with you—it is dark and you may lose your footing.'

The wine! Lee felt her heart contract uneasily. The first weeks after the vintage were fraught with tension and anxieties. But what could she do? She knew little about the fermentation process, and certainly not enough to advise Pierre, who had been making wine before she was born.

As she hurried in the housekeeper's wake she wondered if this unexpected show of anxiety about her condition meant that the cold war the woman had been waging was at an end. She certainly hoped so. Once or twice lately she had come close to suggesting to Gilles that they dispensed with her services altogether, but each time she remembered that the woman had no other home apart from the château. Now she was glad that she had kept silent.

Lee had not been in the cellars since the vintage. Even though the afternoon had been cool and she was wearing a thick cardigan she shivered convulsively as she stepped out of the sunlight into the cold murkiness within. Even the electric light the housekeeper snapped on did little to banish Lee's growing feeling of apprehension. She told herself that she was being foolish, but the moment the huge wooden door swung to behind them, she had an instinctive and overwhelming urge to push it open again and admit the daylight.

There was no sign of Pierre in the main cellar which housed the huge vats of wine. Madame Le Bon made her way unerringly past them, pausing to wait for Lee who was following her reluctantly. The cellars had once extended beneath the entire château, but many of them had been walled up for safety. Even so, when the housekeeper stepped into a narrow, arched tunnel, fear seized Lee by the throat and she longed to turn and run.

'Madame!'

Only the housekeeper's precise, dry voice halted her, and she shivered as she skirted dust-encrusted wine racks, barely glancing at their priceless contents, even though those same bottles anywhere else would have aroused all her professional curiosity and excitement.

Something moved on the cellar floor, and she bit back a scream.

'Alors, these mice!' the housekeeper commented, unmoved. 'Pierre must get himself a cat.'

Mice! Lee cringed. She wasn't really frightened of the small, furry creatures, but there was something about the combination of being so far underground, the long shadows cast by the single dim electric bulb, and the unidentifiable scuttering noises that destroyed her normal calm, good sense.

'Surely Pierre can't be down here?' she protested when the housekeeper unlocked an arched wooden door at the end of the passage and stood aside for Lee to precede her. 'I think you must have it wrong, and he's waiting for me in the château.'

'Non. He said you were to meet him down here,' the housekeeper assured her firmly, as Lee stepped hesitantly into the small room beyond the door.

It was completely empty, but by the time Lee's eyes had grown sufficiently accustomed to the dark to perceive this for themselves, it was too late. The huge door had closed behind her, and as she stood there, frozen with disbelief, she heard the housekeeper turning the key in the lock.

'Now, Madame la Comtesse, let us see if you still as determined to remain at the château!' Lee heard her call triumphantly, the sound flattened by the thick wood. 'You may call all you wish,' she added callously when Lee begged her to open the door. 'No one ever comes down here.'

The door was too thick for Lee to hear the sound of her retreating footsteps, but her imagination painted the picture vividly enough. Shivering with fear and horror, Lee felt the darkness press down on her, stifling her with the threat of all the unrecognisable horrors it might conceal. All her childhood fears of the dark came rushing back in a wave which made her claw frantically at the wood, even though logic told her that it was an impassable barrier. Only when her nails were broken and her fingers torn did she drop numbly to the cold stone floor of the cellar, her head cradled on her arms as she gave way to her terror. What would happen to her? Had the housekeeper gone mad? Did she intend to leave her down here for the rest of her life? Now, when it was too late, Lee remembered the untouched dust on the bottles and the passage floor. People used that passage seldom, if ever. She could die here and no one would ever know. She must not give way to hysteria. Of course she would be found. The housekeeper was just playing a cruel trick on her, thought up no doubt by Louise. A trick to frighten her into leaving the château... If she was ever allowed to leave it alive. Gilles was away, but in view of their situation he would not be entirely surprised to return and find her gone, her clothes packed and taken away somewhere by Louise and her ally. It would be a simple matter for them to invent a phone call, and a taxi. No one would ever be any the wiser...until it was far too late.

Lee stifled a small sob. For all she knew the woman could be on the other side of that door, listening for signs that she was giving way to her fear. Something scuttled past her feet, and she jumped up with a terrified scream. Shaking and trembling, she backed away from the door, stopping only when she felt the cold roughness of the stone wall behind her. She was going to die, alone in this black prison which embodied all her worst nightmares.

Suddenly the baby kicked, and as she covered the small movement instinctively Lee felt her terror die away. She was being foolish, Louise might want Gilles, but she would hardly go to the lengths of committing murder to get him. No, all she probably intended to do was to give Lee a fright; force her into fleeing the château, preferably before Gilles returned. The phone call and the taxi were probably very much a part of Louise's plan, but real and not fictional. All she had to do was keep calm and simply wait. The darkness which was so terrifying could not hurt her. It held no horrors; no fearsome creatures waiting to destroy her. Forcing herself to keep calm, she made her way blindly round the small room, touching the cold stones, and dismayed at one point to find them damp, running with a trickle of water. The room was about six feet square. She paced it slowly, telling herself that any small creatures she might disturb would be far more terrified of her than she needed to be of them.

It was growing colder by the minute and she forced herself to keep walking, swinging her arms to try and keep warm, and trying not to remember all the appallingly sad stories she had ever read about people imprisoned in the Bastille, sometimes for an entire lifetime.

She licked her lips. They were dry. She felt very thirsty—and hungry. How long had she been down here? One hour? Two? She had no way of knowing; no means of discovering how long Louise intended to draw out her torture. Remembering the look on the Frenchwoman's face at the end of their last interview, Lee reflected that she would not be inclined to be merciful. The baby moved again, and she was filled with a fresh fear.

All the growing love she had felt for Gilles' child during the months she had been carrying it crystallised in a surge of protective fear, and she suddenly realised what high stakes Louise was gambling for. If she did not leave as Louise must hope, and told Gilles what had happened, it must surely mean an end to Louise's chances of reinstating herself in Gilles' life?

Gilles might not care what happened to *her*. But he did care about his child—passionately!

Fresh tears welled, as the panic she was trying to bank down welled up and her hands reached convulsively for the locked door. She banged on it frantically, waiting in a silence that tortured her eardrums for some sort of response, shouting until she was hoarse, in the forlorn hope that someone might actually venture down here and be alerted to her plight. Not for nothing did Madame Le Bon carry all the household keys, and now, when it was too late, Lee remembered that she had actually had to unlock the door leading to the passage—something which surely would not have been necessary were the cellar in constant usage. Her thoughts rushed backwards and forwards, tormenting her until her head ached with the effort of trying to think. She stopped pacing for a moment and realised that she was shivering with cold, her fingers already almost numb. She reached for the door again and then slumped back forlornly. What was the use? No one was going to hear her. Tears welled and she sank to the floor, curling up into a small ball, listening for the longed-for sound of another human being, until exhaustion claimed her and she fell into an uneasy sleep.

'YOU SAY LEE is missing, but where can she have gone?' Marie-Thérèse was puzzled. It was true that she had not warned Lee that she might visit her, but with Gilles away in Paris she had thought Lee might be lonely, but now the housekeeper was telling her that Lee was not in the château.

'Not gone, but missing,' the cook protested fiercely. All three of them were in the kitchen, where Marie-Thérèse had gone thinking she might find Lee. 'Madame was not in her room when Claire took up her tea,' she told Marie-Thérèse. 'Always she lets me know if there is to be any change, but today, nothing. She is missing Monsieur le Comte and has perhaps wandered away from the château. Every afternoon she walks, but always she has returned by this time.'

'Have you looked for her?' Marie-Thérèse demanded worriedly. The cook's words had reactivated her own fears that Lee had something on her mind, and might have been less careful than she would normally be. Anything could have happened to her.

The housekeeper shrugged sourly.

'Madame la Comtesse is mistress here, it is not for us to question her whereabouts.'

'But she did not tell you she was going out,' Marie-Thérèse insisted, 'and now she cannot be found?' When the housekeeper did not answer she walked purposefully towards the door. 'I am going to telephone Monsieur le Comte and my husband. We must search the house and land for Madame.' She held out her hand to the housekeeper. 'I shall take the keys and go through every room. You will organise the men to search the gardens and fields.'

Marie-Thérèse nearly lost her temper when the woman appeared reluctant to part with her keys. Her manner was so surly that she did not trust her to search the rooms herself. It was almost as though she wanted some misfortune to befall Lee, she thought anxiously, her heart missing a beat.

Jean-Paul managed to get hold of Gilles by telephoning first his hotel, and then the Ministry, who eventually tracked him down at a reception.

When he came to the phone his voice was curt, but when Jean-Paul outlined the position, he announced that he was returning immediately.

When he had hung up Gilles did not immediately leave the luxurious study of his host, but instead stared unseeingly out on to the wide, gracious Faubourg, his face taut and white.

'Gilles!' The Minister stopped dead as he observed his face. 'Is something wrong?'

'A personal matter.' The words were terse. 'I must leave immediately, but first, may I use your phone? I have a couple of calls to make.'

The Minister agreed instantly and when he had gone Gilles picked up the receiver. There was only one taxi firm in Chauvigny, and the Paris train stopped there twice a day. When he had assured himself that Lee had not made use of either of these escape routes, he took a taxi, to his hotel, and within half an hour of receiving Jean-Paul's call was on his way back to Chauvigny, driving down the long, straight roads at a speed which—even for a Frenchman—bordered on the suicidal.

The moment he pulled up in the courtyard the door opened, his drawn face illuminated in the beam of light as he demanded curtly, 'Have you found her?'

Jean-Paul shook his head. He had been dreading this moment, trying to put himself in his friend's place. Gilles' self-control was phenomenal, but maintaining it had drawn grooves either side of his mouth and thrust into prominence the bones of his face, making it all planes and angles.

'We have searched everywhere. I have sent Marie-Thérèse home, but the men and I have combed the fields, the wood, the house, even the wine cellar.'

'Madame would never go down there alone,' Pierre interrupted positively. When Gilles frowned he shrugged apologetically. 'Forgive me, but I could not help but notice her reaction when she came down once with Jean-Paul. She tried to hide it, but she was frightened. It is being underground—it affects some people like that.'

'And no one has seen her? No one at all? Summon all the staff,' Gilles instructed Pierre tersely. 'She cannot have simply disappeared. Someone must have seen something.'

'We have talked to them already, Gilles,' Jean-Paul said gently. 'The last time she was seen was during the afternoon. She was walking in the garden with Madame Le Bon.'

Gilles turned to the housekeeper.

'What time was this?'

She replied as calmly as she could. When she locked Lee in the cellar all she had intended to do was to frighten her into leaving the château as Madame Louise had planned, but Marie-Thérèse had taken the keys from her and now Jean-Paul had them, and she was too terrified to admit that she had.

'We will search again,' Gilles decided. 'The château is a large house and it is possible that something may have been overlooked on the first occasion.'

Jean-Paul shook his head compassionately. 'Do you not think it would be wiser to alert the police, *mon ami*?' he suggested, but Gilles shook his head.

'If you will go through the château, Pierre and I will search outside. I see you already have the keys.'

Jean-Paul nodded. 'Yes, but Marie-Thérèse could not find doors to fit these.'

He held up two keys, and Pierre stepped forward, examining them frowningly.

'These open the door to the cellar where we keep the old wines, and the small one beyond it that is no longer in use.'

'Has anyone searched them?' Gilles' voice was clipped. No one noticed Madame Le Bon pale and shake visibly at his question.

Pierre scratched his head. 'But she cannot be down there! There is no reason…'

Gilles strode out before he could finish, Jean-Paul hot on his heels.

In her haste Madame Le Bon had neglected to lock the door to the wine cellar behind her, and it swung open at Gilles' touch, the solitary light bulb which had cast such horrifying shadows for Lee clearly illuminating the dusty bottles.

'Someone has been down here.' Gilles was studying the bottle Lee had leaned against when the mouse frightened her. 'Give me the keys for the store-room,' he demanded tersely.

Jean-Paul and Pierre hung back as Gilles unlocked the wooden door. How on earth could Lee be down here? The door swung open and in the darkness they could see nothing, except Gilles' back as he bent down and slowly lifted something into his arms. 'Call the doctor,' he commanded curtly.

LEE WAS COLD. Not just cold, but frozen. She had been warm, drifting in a soft safe world, but someone was trying to drag her away from it. She protested soundlessly, twisting away from the hard fingers on her shoulder, and then all at once the reality she had been trying so hard to forget burst upon her. She cried protestingly, blinking in the electric light as she opened her eyes, relief flooding through her as she realised that she was no longer locked up in that terrifying dark prison from which she had thought she would never escape.

'Gilles!'

The man carrying her stopped and Lee realised for the first time that the arms holding her so securely were those of her husband. Weak tears rolled down her cheeks, making fresh tracks on her dusty skin.

'Madame Le Bon locked me in,' she tried to say, but her throat was too sore and the words would not come.

'Hush, *chérie*,' Gilles soothed. 'You are quite safe now. I am taking you to your room, and we have sent for the doctor. We will talk about it later when you are rested.'

Lee needed no second bidding; it was a relief to relax and close her eyes, listening to the reassuring thud of Gilles' heart. She felt no inclination to move away from him, or demand that he set her free, and when he placed her on their bed and closed the door behind him, she watched him with eyes still dark and shadowed with suffering, making no protest when he started to remove her filthy clothes, with hands so gentle that his touch brought fresh tears. Her skin was scraped where she had bumped into the rough stone walls, dried blood matted with the dust that covered her flesh.

From a distance she heard Gilles swear and when she opened her eyes his face was bone-white.

'Lie still,' he commanded softly. 'I am just going to get some water to bathe your cuts, and then we will let the doctor look at them.'

In the event there wasn't time. The doctor was ushered into the room before Gilles had returned from the bathroom. His matter-of-fact attitude did much to alleviate Lee's sense of unreality. She had suffered no apparent injury, he told Gilles, who explained that she had been trapped in the cellar, but he would prescribe something for shock just in case.

'No drugs,' Lee protested, the effort of speaking taxing her slender store of strength. There was one question she had to ask the doctor, and her eyes appealed to Gilles for help.

When he bent down over the bed, his ear close to

her lips, she managed to whisper tremulously, 'The baby.'

Tears shimmered in her eyes as she thought of the small, helpless life inside her, and for a moment Gilles' profile wavered, an expression she found it hard to interpret in the grey eyes. She could almost have described it as bitter, haunted even, but she was too exhausted to dwell deeply on it.

'Your baby is fine,' the doctor assured her with a beam. 'Indeed he has come off far better than his mother, although you must rest properly for a couple of days.'

Gilles turned to follow the doctor as he left the room, snapping off the light, and Lee could not prevent herself from calling out in a panic as the blackness engulfed her. Gilles was at her side instantly.

'Your wife has had an unpleasant experience, *monsieur*,' the doctor commented, 'but better than any medicine I can prescribe is the presence of her husband at her side. I shall see myself out.'

When he had gone a curious silence seemed to fall over the room.

'Are you feeling well enough to tell me what happened?' Gilles asked. He was sitting on the edge of the bed, his shoulders broad beneath his thin silk shirt, his eyes shadowed.

Haltingly, her voice almost failing her at times, Lee described what had happened without implicating Louise. That was for Gilles to discover, if he wished, and she thought it significant that although his eyes darkened ominously when she described how Ma-

dame Le Bon had left her, he made no comment as
to why the woman should have acted in so dangerous
a fashion.

A knock on the door heralded the arrival of a maid
with a supper tray, and when she had put it down,
Lee became conscious of her grubby bedraggled state.

'I should like to wash…' she began hesitantly.

'I'll go downstairs and get one of the maids to
come up and help you.'

He moved towards the door. In a moment he would
be gone and she would be alone. Lee shivered, swept
by the terror which had engulfed her in the cellar.

'Don't leave me!'

Gilles stared at her, but Lee was beyond wondering
what her words might reveal. Her fingers curled into
small desperate fists as he watched her. 'Don't leave
me, Gilles,' she begged. 'I'm so frightened!'

The tears she had tried to stem during her imprisonment ran unchecked down her face, her shoulders
shaking soundlessly. With a muffled imprecation
Gilles crossed the space dividing them, lifting her up
into his arms and carrying her into the bathroom.

'I won't leave you,' he promised soothingly, 'but
we must clean these wounds. Shall I do it for you? I
have never been a lady's maid before, so you will
have to be patient with me if I am clumsy.' Lee recognised dimly that the gentle even pitch of his voice
was deliberately adopted to stem her hysteria, and that
if she had any pride she would banish him and wash
herself. She was not helpless, after all, but every time
she opened her mouth to do so she would remember

the cellar and a fresh surge of weakness would rob her of the ability to do anything but gratefully accept his tender ministrations.

'Lee, be truthful with me,' he said at one point, kneeling in front of her while he applied antiseptic to her scraped knees. 'Just then when you asked the doctor about the baby, I got the impression that you genuinely cared about the child.'

Lee bit her lip. How blind he was! Of course she cared about her baby. After him it was the most important thing in her life.

'Lee, I know the circumstances of our marriage have not been ideal, but we are married, for better or for worse, and we have a joint responsibility to the child we have created jointly.' He paused as though searching for the right words, and Lee, who had never seen him at a loss before, felt her heart melt with tenderness. He was so close—close enough for her to reach out and touch—and yet so remote. She could touch his flesh, but not his heart.

'For the child's sake cannot we call a truce? I give you my word that I shall not force my...attentions upon you, nor will I embarrass you with liaisons such as the one I had with Louise, and in return...' He stood up abruptly, grasping her hands and looking into her eyes. 'In return I ask only that you love our child. Well, Lee? Do we have a truce?'

What could she say? That it was unfair of him to ask this of her now, when her defences had crumbled, when her heart ached for tenderness and her body for his protection?

Her heart cried out that what he was suggesting was not enough, that one day there would come a time when she could no longer endure the sterile relationship he was advocating; a day when she would either have to beg for his love or remove herself from his life, but she was too exhausted to wage war against her own clamouring senses, who demanded that she take whatever crumbs he was prepared to offer.

'We have a truce.' The words were so low; so painful that Gilles had to bend his head to catch them. She leaned against him like an exhausted child as he wrapped her in a soft, fluffy towel and carried her back to the bedroom.

A glass of wine was presented to her and she took a few cautious sips.

'It will help you sleep,' Gilles told her, coaxing her to drink a little more. 'Try to eat a little of this salad while I make a phone call.'

There was a phone in the room, and listening to him apologise for his unscheduled departure from the Ministry guilt washed over her.

'I've caused you a lot of trouble.'

'Indeed you have.' The enigmatic smile hurt more than the words, because she had the feeling that there was some meaning behind it that was hidden from her.

'I would have returned tomorrow anyway,' Gilles assured her. 'Lee, before you go back to sleep there is something we must talk about. Although you have not mentioned her I recognise Louise's hand behind your imprisonment.' His mouth tightened and Lee knew that there would be no compassion for the woman who had once been his mistress. 'It is unfortunate that circumstances prevent me from taxing Louise openly with her infamy, but you may rest assured that she will not be left in doubt as to my feelings, and I shall suggest strongly to her father that it is time she returned to Paris—for good.'

'And Madame Le Bon?'

'She left, apparently, while we were down in the cellars. Do you wish to have her pursued?'

Lee shook her head.

'What would be the point? I don't think she meant to leave me down there.' She would not tell him of her foolish imaginings—it was over now, and she suspected that Madame Le Bon had been punished enough by the realisation that she had almost caused a tragedy. It was Louise who was really to blame— not the woman she had used as her tool.

'Try and sleep now,' Gilles told her, when she had finished picking at her food. 'I shall only be in the dressing room. I shall work for a while and then go to bed, but I shall be here all the time if you need me.'

Gilles had been sleeping in the dressing room ever since the night of the ball. No one had commented on it, and Lee assumed that if the staff were aware of it—and they must be—they would put it down to her pregnancy. Pregnant women were notorious for their strange fancies.

The wine helped to relax her tensed muscles, the

sounds of Gilles moving about in the dressing room soothing her into sleep.

SHE WAS DREAMING… She was shut in a dark room, and although she called and called, no one came to set her free. The darkness seemed to press in on her, and although she begged Louise to let her out, the other woman only laughed callously. 'I'll go away,' Lee promised. 'I'll never come back.' But the Frenchwoman took no notice. She came closer and closer, her red hair curling round her face like flames, her mouth cruel as she told Lee that she would never, never be free.

The dream faded as Gilles shook her awake, and it came as a shock to realise that the sobbing she had heard so dimly in her dream had been her own. Her body was drenched with perspiration and yet she still felt dreadfully cold. Her teeth were chattering, and even in the darkness she could see the grim anger in Gilles' eyes. She flinched beneath it, apologising huskily for wakening him.

'I wasn't asleep,' he told her abruptly. 'Lee, did you think Louise intended you to say down there for ever?'

She passed her tongue over her dry lips, not wanting him to think her hysterically stupid.

'It did cross my mind, but not very seriously. I think she just wanted to frighten me.'

'Into leaving the château? That's what you said during your nightmare.'

'It wasn't just because of Louise, I've always been

frightened of the dark.' She shuddered suddenly, remembering the cellar, and as though he read her mind and saw the horror etched there, Gilles took her in his arms. As she felt the dampness of his skin against her, Lee realised that she must have disturbed him while he was having a shower. Her eyes went to his hair, dark, and still wet, sliding lower to his shoulders, his skin gleaming like oiled silk, and longing rose up inside her like spring floods after the thaw.

His hand smoothed the tangled hair back off her forehead, his eyes searching her face.

'Will you be all right now?'

His voice was faintly husky, his hands withdrawn from her body, and she shivered again, her fingers trembling yearningly against his chest as she reached towards him.

'Gilles, don't leave me.' The words were a repeat of those she had murmured earlier, but this time with a different meaning, and Lee could not bring herself to look at him, as she realised what she had said. 'I'm so cold,' she temporised, 'and frightened.' Neither were lies, but overriding them both was the need to have him beside her, his arms around her, even if it was only to protect her from her own childish nightmares.

'You want me to stay?' His eyes probed her shadowed features. 'You're very trusting, Lee. Or are you testing me to see if I can keep my word? Don't worry, you're quite safe.'

But did she want to be? Lee thought drowsily as he slid into the bed beside her, turning her into the warmth of his own body, the touch of his flesh sending her pulses out of control, flooding her with a desire more powerful than all her earlier fears.

There was a moment when, on the edge of sleep, she thought she felt the light brush of Gilles' lips against her hair, but the caress was not repeated and she thought she must have imagined it, until she felt Gilles' breath stir her hair.

'We haven't sealed our bargain,' he reminded her, and her heart pounded heavily at the sensual undertone to the words. 'Trust will be the cornerstone of our relationship, Lee. Do you trust me?'

Her mouth had gone dry, and as his touched it lightly she had to take a deep breath to prevent herself from shaking. His lips moved softly over hers, brushing them with a sensual expertise that left her longing to prolong the kiss.

'Trust me, Lee,' he murmured against her skin. His hands stroked the soft skin of her shoulders, sliding into her hair to tilt her head back, as his lips touched hers again. There was no force, no passion, just gentle warmth, and although Lee knew he had intended to reassure her, her predominant feeling was one of intense disappointment. What had she expected? That the moment he touched her desire would flare into life and that he would not be able to stop himself from making love to her? She smiled wryly. That was the stuff of romances, not life.

When he released her she veiled her eyes from him automatically, not wanting him to read what she felt must be reflected there.

'You see?' There was a smile in his voice. 'I can behave in a civilised manner!'

But it was the pagan in him that called to her, Lee acknowledged; the Gilles who had possessed her beneath a canopy of trees, while the rain drummed into the parched earth, and for a moment they had been at one with the universe, elemental and almost divine. If only she could stay within the haven of his arms for the rest of her life, feeling the powerful beat of his heart against her flesh, breathing in the warm male scent of his body, and feeling her own relax gradually from fear.

She closed her eyes hesitantly, but Gilles' arms held at bay the nightmares which had tormented her earlier.

This time, when she slept, it was dreamlessly.

CHAPTER TEN

LEE examined her reflection nervously in the mirror She would have given anything to avoid going to this party. Gilles had watched her closely when he told her about the invitation. It was Monsieur Trouville rather than Louise, but all the same the Frenchwoman would be there. And if they did not go, Louise would know why; she would know that Lee still remembered her ordeal in the cellar, and Lee was determined not to give her that satisfaction. And besides, she knew that Gilles was extremely fond of Louise's father. Although he had sold most of his land to Gilles, he intended to remain in the area, and they could not spend the rest of their lives pretending that he did not exist.

The worst thing would be facing Louise as though nothing had happened; pretending that the whole thing had merely been an unfortunate accident, which was the story Gilles had allowed to circulate locally. Madame Le Bon had completely disappeared; she had relatives in Paris and Lee suspected she must have gone there.

One good thing to come out of the incident was Gilles' changed manner towards her. Lee never had to sleep alone in the huge bed now, and if she woke up during the night, Gilles always seemed to be aware of it, drawing her next to the protective warmth of his own body, sometimes without even opening his eyes—but that was all. He might have been a father indulging a small child for all the interest he took in her sexually.

They had driven into Nantes for her check-up the previous day and the doctor had been very pleased with her progress, although he warned her that she was still a little underweight. Gilles had insisted on buying her a new dress, a rich burgundy velvet, gathered gently at the front from a curved yoke, with a cream lace collar and cuffs. It suited her, bringing out the rich colour of her hair, which she was just twisting into a smooth chignon when Gilles opened the bedroom door. He halted and watched her, an expression in her eyes she found hard to define. He had been working hard and looked tired, and she longed to walk into his arms and smooth the frown from between his eyes.

'Are you sure you want to do this, Lee? You don't have to, you know.'

'I know.' She had to swallow hard on the tears which had gathered at the back of her throat in a hard lump, forcing herself to say gaily, 'But have you ever heard of a woman refusing to attend a party?'

It was being held to celebrate the New Year, and as they drove through Chauvigny, Lee couldn't help wondering exactly what that year might hold for her. She looked at Gilles. His hands held the wheel firmly, his attention concentrated on the road. His hair brushed the collar of his burgundy velvet jacket and

she had to stifle an impulse to touch it, burying her
fingers in its thick softness. His shirt glimmered
palely in the dark, and a melting weakness invaded
her stomach. If only this was a real marriage; the sort
of marriage where she could turn to him and tell him
to stop the car and take her home, where they could
be alone to welcome in the New Year in the only way
she really wanted to—held fast in his arms. Her small
half sigh caught his attention and he glanced towards
her.

'Are you sure you want to go?'

Lee smiled wryly. 'Not really, but it's something I
must do, Gilles. Louise isn't going to simply disappear because I want her to. Sooner or later I shall
have to face her.'

The hands gripping the steering wheel tightened
perceptibly. 'When I think of what might have happened...' His face had gone white. For a man of such
self-control his feelings for his unborn child never
ceased to amaze her, Lee thought a little jealously.
Their child would never lack a father's love. Nor a
mother's, she promised herself, and yet in her heart
she knew for her own sake that she ought to leave
before she betrayed herself and changed Gilles' kind
tolerance into contempt for her unwanted love.

Louise welcomed them enthusiastically, her eyes
on the emerald earrings Gilles had given to Lee with
her Christmas present.

'Somewhat premature, surely?' was her only comment, but there was a hard challenge in her eyes that
made Lee glad of Gilles' lean bulk between them.

'On the contrary,' Gilles replied smoothly, 'I had intended to give them to Lee before.'

'You are a very lucky woman. They must be worth a fortune. Aren't you frightened something might happen to them?'

The gloves were off with a vengeance, Lee reflected, trying to appear unmoved by Louise's enmity. Hatred had gleamed in her eyes as she looked at the emeralds, and it was all Lee could do to prevent herself from trembling visibly when she remembered the cold darkness of the cellar.

Gilles answered for her, his arm curved protectively round her body, the look in his eyes tender and reassuring. He was an excellent actor, she thought, not for the first time.

'What could happen?' Gilles asked evenly. 'Surely you aren't suggesting that some of your guests are…dishonest?'

Louise shrugged, but her eyes were hard. She knew and they knew that they were not merely discussing the emeralds. They were soon swallowed up among the other guests. Someone found Lee a chair, and she found that her French had improved sufficiently for her to be able to hold her own in the conversation. When Gilles murmured that he wanted to have a word with Louise's father, she felt a momentary pang of fear, but she quelled it immediately. Gilles could not be at her side every moment of her life, and Louise could scarcely harm her here!

She ought to have known better. A buffet had been set out in the dining room, and Lee waited until most people had eaten before going to fill her own plate.

She passed Gilles, who was still talking, and he acknowledged her presence with a small smile. His attentive care was becoming more of a burden than his indifference had ever been. So many times she had been dangerously close to allowing herself to believe he genuinely cared about her; dangerously close to deceiving herself that his touch was that of a lover and not merely a man concerned for the life of his unborn child.

Louise walked into the dining room as Lee was on her way out and they met by the door, Lee clamping down on her instinctive fear. Louise smiled cruelly.

'Ah, there you are—I was looking for you. Lee, we have another guest—an old friend of yours who has only just arrived.'

For the first time Lee noticed the man standing in the shadows behind her, his fair hair catching the light.

'Drew!' Shock stifled her, her eyes dilating as she stared up into the cold features of the man she had once thought she loved.

He stared back at her, grimacing distastefully as his glance lingered on her body.

'Wh-what are you doing here?'

Lee realised immediately that the question was a foolish one, smacking of guilt, and Drew's expression mirrored her fears.

'I came because I thought I might be able to persuade you to come to your senses,' he began angrily. 'When I got your letter breaking off our engagement, I thought you were simply having second thoughts.'

His mouth went tight with distaste, and he turned to Louise, who had been watching gleefully.

'I have to thank you for your warning.' His lip curled faintly as he looked at Lee. 'A little previous, weren't you, or were you hoping to persuade your lover into marrying you? My God, and to think I kept my hands off you because I thought you were different? If I'd known...'

Lee had listened to him in growing disgust and fury, and now it overwhelmed her.

'If you'd known, you would have what?' she demanded angrily. 'Had a brief affair with me instead of "buying" my virginity with an engagement ring?'.

She felt sickened by the realisation that Drew had simply wanted her because he had thought her a rare commodity. Her innocence had been something he thought he could buy and parade proudly in front of his family. Had she admitted to any previous affairs he would never have contemplated becoming engaged to her, she realised with hindsight, remembering their earlier conversations, his questions about her background and past, which she had answered guilelessly merely thinking that he was interested in her as she had been in him. Now she knew better, and looking into his face she felt only relief that she had been spared marriage to him.

'At least you had the decency to break off our engagement, although I suppose you thought you'd left it a bit late to pass the child off as mine.'

Lee's face went white. She couldn't believe that this was the same man who had only a year before had professed to love her. She swayed and closed her eyes, catching her breath as she felt a hard arm supporting her.

'Gilles!' He must have seen them from the drawing room.

Drew was looking at him with cold dislike. 'I wish you joy of her,' he said maliciously. 'Although by the looks of her, you've already had it.'

Louise screamed as Gilles' fist connected with Drew's jaw. For a moment he didn't move, staring at Gilles in stunned surprise, before crumpling slowly to the floor.

'Gilles, how could you!' Louise protested. 'He was within his rights. Did you know that Lee was engaged to him at the time she married you?' Her voice suggested that she thought he had not.

'I knew,' Gilles said grimly. 'Why do you think I was so anxious to tie her to me? But what I don't know is what he is doing here.' He glanced curtly down at Drew's unconscious figure. 'However, I can guess. This is the last time you interfere in my affairs, Louise, and much as I respect your father, I am inclined to tell him exactly what sort of woman he has for a daughter. Your husband did not leave you very well off, I believe,' he said pleasantly, 'and your father is extremely generous. Take care, Louise.'

Drew had come round and sat on the floor nursing his swollen jaw, his expression belligerent.

'I'll sue!' he threatened Gilles, allowing Louise to help him to his feet.

'Try it,' was Gilles' grim rejoinder. 'There isn't a court in France that will support your action. A man is entitled to defend his wife's honour.'

'His wife?' Drew stared disbelievingly at Lee, and then turned accusingly to Louise. 'You didn't tell me he'd married her!'

Lee didn't need to ask how Louise had obtained Drew's address—or why. She must have seen the letter Lee had written to him, and had perhaps thought when her earlier plan failed that Drew's arrival might turn Gilles back to herself. Louise had no way of knowing that Gilles knew all about Drew, and was hardly likely to be jealous of the other man, even had Lee had an intensely passionate relationship with him.

'Well, you're welcome to her,' Drew sneered, glowering at Gilles. 'Personally, I'm not very keen on other men's leavings.'

'It is just as well that I'm not a violent man,' Gilles replied smoothly. 'And that I know your remarks spring purely from jealousy. As I have every reason to know, your insults are entirely unfounded, and even if they weren't...' The look in his eyes made the colour come and go in Lee's cheeks. 'I have loved Lee since she was sixteen,' Gilles said softly, 'and nothing anyone could say about her could lessen that love.' He turned to Louise. 'It doesn't take much imagination to guess what you had in mind. I'm sorry to have to say this, Louise, but even if you had succeeded; even if Lee had left me, there is no place in my life for you.'

As he guided her out, Lee had time to feel almost sorry for Louise.

Gilles opened the car door and saw that she was comfortable before taking his own seat. He started the engine without a word, and when Lee looked at him she saw that there was a hard white line round his lips as though he was in the grip of some intense emotion.

'I'm sorry you had to go through that,' he said abruptly. 'Louise is a first-class bitch.'

Lee shrugged tiredly, 'It doesn't matter.' All at once reaction set in and to her shame, tears started to roll down her cheeks. Gilles swore and stopped the car, proffering an immaculate handkerchief, but the tears would not stop. They were only a few miles from the château and Gilles re-started the car, driving faster than usual, his expression withdrawn as he brought the Mercedes to a halt in front of the house.

Lee didn't wait for him to open her door. All at once the insults Drew had thrown at her broke through the calm she had exercised in his presence, and she felt almost unclean. This was the man she had once thought she loved and intended to spend her whole life with; a man so shallow and vindictive that he had wanted to destroy her rather than let her find happiness elsewhere; a man who wanted her only because of what she represented.

She could hear Gilles calling her name, but she did not stop. She wanted to be alone, to let the cleansing tears flow and wash away the memory of Drew's words.

Pierre stopped Gilles in the hall, and Lee escaped to the privacy of their bedroom, flinging herself down on the bed and giving way to the emotional storm she had been damming up ever since her release from the cellar. Gilles' kindness to her had meant that her emotions had had to be kept strictly under control, her senses alert for every danger to the fragile peace which existed between them.

'Lee.' She let Gilles turn her over, and survey her tear-damp face. 'I could kill him for this,' he told her harshly. 'And Louise. I suppose there's no point in telling you that he wouldn't have made you happy, that he wanted you only as a possession.'

His arms were hard and warm. He had removed his jacket and Lee burrowed instinctively against the warmth of his chest, murmuring an inarticulate protest, as the thin silk shirt prevented her from achieving the closeness she craved. She clung blindly to Gilles as he rocked her gently, all her good intentions forgotten as longing swept her and her fingers moved of their own accord to the small pearl buttons, unfastening them and laying bare the moist heat of the flesh beneath. Her hands spread out feverishly, feeling the steady beat of his heart, the faint rasp of his body hair beneath her sensitive fingertips. She closed her eyes, trembling with the need she could no longer deny, her lips dry as she pressed them lightly against his throat.

His arms tightened; he pulled her on to his knee, his fingers stroking her softly.

'Gilles?' She lifted her face in mute invitation, no longer caring what she was revealing, pressing her body against him as she sought the possession of his kiss.

'Lee, don't make it harder for me,' he begged harshly. 'Leave me at least some dignity. If I don't leave now, I'll never be able to let you go, and although I promised you I'd never force myself on you again, I'm dreadfully close to breaking that promise. Oh God, *Lee*!'

There was a raw hunger in his voice that brought her from bitter despair to disbelieving incredulity. He groaned suddenly, finding her mouth with his own and possessing it with an urgency that swept aside all barriers. Lee clung to him with an abandon she was barely aware of, murmuring soft, incoherent cries of delight as his mouth moved from her lips to the soft creamy flesh his trembling fingers had exposed.

'Stop me, Lee,' he groaned at one point, his face flushed with the desire he was making no attempt to conceal. 'Stop me before it's too late.'

'I don't want to.'

The whispered confession stilled his questing hands. He looked at her for a moment, breathing as though the effort pained him, and then cupped her flushed cheeks, his voice unsteady as he muttered huskily, 'I told myself I'd never do this; never sink to emotional blackmail; that I'd never burden you with my feelings, but I didn't know then how desperate I would become. Stay with me, Lee. Let me teach you to love me. Perhaps you'll never be able to love me the way I love you, but you aren't indifferent to me.' His fingers tilted her chin upwards, the look in his eyes making her heart lift on a cresting wave of delirious happiness.

'That day when we made love for the first time was the most memorable of my entire life. I had convinced myself that you were just another woman— desirable, but nothing more. I kept reminding myself that you had disillusioned me once, that you were no different from any other woman. I had forced you into marriage, but it wasn't enough. I was tormented every time I touched you by the thought of all the other men who had known you before me. I wanted to possess you completely, an illogical desire which I could not equate with common sense. And then when I discovered that I had been wrong! I cannot describe to you how I felt, how much I loathed and despised myself, and yet even knowing what I had done didn't stop me from wanting you. I hated myself and I swore I wouldn't force myself upon you again, but every time I remembered that evening—and I remembered it constantly—I wanted you more. I couldn't believe it had actually happened. You were a virgin, innocent and inexperienced, and yet with you I experienced something I had known with no other woman—a total blending of minds and bodies. You'll never know how many times since then I've wanted to make you respond to me, to take the physical satisfaction I knew we could have together and pray that love would come, but I couldn't. I told myself I would have to set you free, and then I found out you were carrying my child. Will you hate me if I tell you that I was glad, fiercely glad because it gave me an excuse to hold on to you... Just as Louise gave me an excuse to force you into marrying me.'

'Will you hate me if I tell you that I was glad, that I wanted your child only a little less than I wanted your love?' Lee murmured tremulously.

For a moment there was silence, and then Gilles lowered his head, brushing her lips delicately, running his tongue over them, like a blind man exploring by touch alone, and then as Lee reached up for him he held her away, his eyes searching her face.

'Be very sure, my darling,' he said softly. 'There is nothing to be ashamed of in admitting that I arouse you physically. I am the first lover you have ever known, and you have a deeply passionate nature. I say this because my own love is such that physical passion alone will not be enough to satisfy my burning need for you. I want all of you, Lee, and I warn you now if you stay with me, I will possess you completely, and never set you free.'

'It isn't merely physical,' Lee told him softly. 'I love you, Gilles. Living with you like this has been torture. Every time you touch me I...' She flushed and broke off, her emotion still too tender to be put into words.

'You what?' Gilles prompted softly. 'Or shall I say it for both of us? Every time I look at you, I am consumed by the need to touch you, and when I touch you I want to go on touching you, and have you touch me in return. Like this.'

He drew her into his arms and kissed her tenderly before drawing slightly away, but as he had said, it wasn't enough, and Lee reached urgently for him, her eyes begging him mutely not to let her go. As though he still doubted her love he hesitated, watching her, and Lee knew that there must be no more misunderstandings or doubts. Sliding her hands over his shoulders, she lifted her head, her fingers delicately tracing the smooth muscles of his back as she pressed kisses against the warm column of his throat. She felt him tense and swallow, and her lips parted on a sudden aching wave of love. There was no need for words. His kiss blotted out everything but their mutual need.

A long time later Gilles released her, laughter gleaming in the depths of eyes no longer cold but warm with the intensity of their love.

'If I didn't know better, I might question exactly how you learned to arouse a man so thoroughly.'

'Ask me.' Lee dimpled back at him. 'I'll tell you anyway. I learned from my husband—whom I love very much.'

'And who loves you, but dares not show it at this precise moment in time.' His eyes lingered on the swelling curves of her body, and he smiled humorously. 'For the first time I find myself resenting the presence of our child, but later, after he is born...' His eyes darkened suddenly and he got off the bed.

'I fell in love with you when you were sixteen, that summer I spent at my aunt's. You were a rose in the bud, so perfect, so unawakened. I knew you were attracted to me, but I was a man of twenty odd, and it would have been criminal to put into practice what I was thinking—almost literally,' he added, pointedly. 'But I couldn't stop thinking about you, about how it would feel to teach you all about love, to feel your first shy responses, and later the ardour I knew you were capable of—and then I got that letter.' He glanced at her and grimaced. 'I nearly went out of my mind! You caught me on my most vulnerable spot. I thought of myself as a man of the world, but here I was deceived by a sixteen-year-old girl, who looked like a child and had the knowledge of a woman of the streets. I had to leave. If I'd stayed I would have taken you—I couldn't have stopped myself. It was like an illness, and even though I loathed you, or what I thought was you, I still wanted you. Years passed, and I told myself I'd forgotten, but I hadn't. And then I saw you again, and it all came back, and I still wanted you.'

'I never wrote the letter,' Lee told him drowsily. 'It was Sally. When I read it I didn't understand half the things in it, but later, when you'd gone, I tried to learn, and when I had learned, I was so sickened, so bitterly hurt that you could believe I was like that that I told myself I hated you; that you had destroyed my innocence and opened my eyes to degradation and obscenity.'

Gilles groaned and took her back in his arms.

'Forgive me? It was because I loved you. My love blinded me to the truth. Perhaps I even wanted to think the worst of you, as though in some way that made my desire for you more understandable. What a fool I've been! When you gave yourself to me with such innocent abandon I nearly went out of my mind. When I found you there in the copse I wanted to punish you for frightening me so badly. I thought you had left me, and then when we started to make love my anger possessed me, and I wanted to obliterate from your mind all those men who had known you first. By the time I realised that they were entirely fictional it was far too late to draw back...'

'And I didn't want you to,' Lee said dreamily. 'I thought you were disgusted, shocked by my response... And then you accused me of experimenting...'

'Because I thought you were. I couldn't believe that you might actually care for me, and had you but known it, giving yourself to me like that was the worst punishment you could have devised. I had possessed you, yes, but it wasn't enough, and I knew that no matter what happened in my life those moments would always be my most precious memory. I love you, Lee,' he said huskily, 'far too much to ever let you go. You'll never know what I went through when I heard you were missing. I thought I had lost you, that you had left me, and then when I discovered the truth I wanted to squeeze Louise's throat until there was no breath left inside her. Today when I saw you with Drew, I thought you must love him. I watched him talking to you and saw you go pale. When I heard him insulting you I wanted to tell him what a fool he was, and yet I felt glad. I knew you had too much pride to plead with him, and I thought that knowing that he had never loved you might make you turn to me...'

'And I thought all your tenderness was because you felt sorry for me, and because you wanted our baby. I never dreamed you loved me. I keep thinking I'm imagining it all and that I'm going to wake up—alone...'

Gilles lifted her hand to his lips, pressing a kiss in the soft palm and closing her fingers over it. 'You're never going to wake up anywhere except in my arms,' he promised huskily, his mouth stifling her response as passion flared insistently between them, and he lowered her gently on to the bed.

SIX MONTHS LATER Lee stretched languorously beneath the hot Greek sun. They had been at the villa for three days and already she had slipped into a carelessly lazy routine. She rolled on to her stomach and watched Gilles swim another length of the pool. Corfu was a beautiful island, but so far they had seen little of it, content in their own private world—just the three of them. A small smile curved her lips as she glanced towards the pram beneath the shade of the olive trees. Philippe was still asleep. With any luck they would have another hour before he woke up. The baby was the image of Gilles, and they had called him Louis-Philippe. If she sat up Lee would just be able to see the fluff of black hair covering his scalp. His eyes, at first blue, were now turning grey.

'Wake up, sleepyhead.' Gilles hauled himself out of the pool, dripping water on her heated skin. He grinned down at her, and although she teased him by closing her eyes, Lee was aware of him with every nerve-ending. The villa had a private beach and last night they had swum together from it. The memory of how they had made love afterwards tinged her lips with a smile. Gilles was a pagan, no matter how he might deny it. He had insisted that they swim nude, and although Lee had at first demurred she had given in and delighted in the cool, silky feel of the water against her sunwarmed flesh; later to be replaced by the hard urgency of Gilles' body.

'Do you think he will make a good *vigneron*?' Gilles asked her, peering down at his son.

Lee rolled on to her back and smiled provocatively. 'Of course he will. It's in his blood...'

Gilles looked at her, and Lee knew they were both remembering the night Philippe had been conceived. There had been many other nights of love since then, but none quite so elemental, and Lee knew that Gilles had been holding back a little. The birth had not been an easy one, but this holiday was already restoring her strength and she knew that there would not be many more nights when Gilles would have to temper his passion.

He came and lay down beside her, and she felt his fingers on the hook of her bikini top. She pretended to be asleep and gasped when he suddenly bit her earlobe.

His arms tightened round her and she opened her eyes, loving the feel of his skull beneath her fingers, his hair still wet from his swim.

'What shall we do tonight? There's supposed to be quite a good nightclub down the road, and we could ask the maid to look after Philippe.'

Lee shook her head decisively, touching her tongue delicately to his throat and tasting the salt from the pool.

'I'd rather stay here.'

Gilles smiled at her, and there was devilment as well as comprehension in the smile.

'Didn't the doctor say something about you resting during the afternoon?'

Lee laughed. 'Call that resting?' she teased. 'And besides, Philippe will need feeding soon.' But Gilles' hands were stroking her skin, and she knew as well as he that her protests held no meaning.

'I love you,' Gilles murmured between kisses, 'more than life itself, Lee.'

She could feel the passion throbbing in his body, and knew instinctively that this time there would be no holding back. When he lifted her in his arms and carried her to their bedroom she felt her own desire rise up to match his, their mutual need engulfing them both in a tide which could not be stemmed.

The passion Lee had experienced the day Gilles had taken her virginity had overwhelmed and exalted her, but it was overshadowed now by the knowledge of Gilles' love and the way that knowledge coloured her own reactions to his passionate possession. Outside Louis-Philippe awakened and cried, and then fell silent, as though comprehending that for the moment his parents were oblivious to his hunger.

Harlequin Romance®

Delightful

Affectionate

Romantic

Emotional

Tender

Original

Daring

Riveting

Enchanting

Adventurous

Moving

Harlequin Romance—the
series that has it all!

HROM-G

HARLEQUIN PRESENTS®

HARLEQUIN PRESENTS
men you won't be able to resist
falling in love with...

HARLEQUIN PRESENTS
women who have feelings
just like your own...

HARLEQUIN PRESENTS
powerful passion in
exotic international settings...

HARLEQUIN PRESENTS
intense, dramatic stories that will keep you
turning to the very last page...

HARLEQUIN PRESENTS
The world's bestselling romance series!

**Harlequin®
Historical**

From rugged lawmen and
valiant knights to defiant heiresses
and spirited frontierswomen,
Harlequin Historicals will
capture your imagination with
their dramatic scope, passion
and adventure.

Harlequin Historicals...
they're too good to miss!

HARLEQUIN®

I N T R I G U E®

We'll leave you breathless!

If you've been looking for thrilling tales of
contemporary passion and sensuous love stories
with taut, edge-of-the-seat suspense—
then you'll *love* **Harlequin Intrigue!**

Every month, you'll meet four new heroes
who are guaranteed to make your spine tingle
and your pulse pound. With them you'll enter
into the exciting world of Harlequin Intrigue—
where your life is on the line
and so is your heart!

THAT'S INTRIGUE—DYNAMIC ROMANCE AT ITS BEST!

HARLEQUIN®

I N T R I G U E®

HARLEQUIN®

AMERICAN ◆ ROMANCE®

LOOK FOR OUR FOUR FABULOUS MEN!

Each month some of today's bestselling authors bring
four new fabulous men to Harlequin American Romance.
Whether they're rebel ranchers, millionaire power brokers
or sexy single dads, they're all gallant princes—and
they're all ready to sweep you into lighthearted fantasies
and contemporary fairy tales where anything is possible
and where all your dreams come true!

You don't even have to make a wish…
Harlequin American Romance will grant your every desire!

Look for Harlequin American Romance
wherever Harlequin books are sold!